The Curse of Eve
and other stories

The Curse of Eve
and other stories

Liliana Blum

Translated from the Spanish by
Toshiya Kamei

Host Publications
Austin, TX

Host Publications, Inc. 277 Broadway, Suite 210, New York, NY 10007

Layout and Design: Joe Bratcher & Anand Ramaswamy
Cover Art: Gabriel Navar
Jacket Design: Anand Ramaswamy

First Edition

Library of Congress Cataloging-in-Publication Data

Blum, Liliana V., 1974-
The curse of Eve and other stories / Liliana Blum ; translated from the Spanish by Toshiya Kamei.
    p. cm.
ISBN-13: 978-0-924047-53-4 (hardcover : alk. paper)
ISBN-10: 0-924047-53-4 (hardcover : alk. paper)
ISBN-13: 978-0-924047-54-1 (pbk. : alk. paper)
ISBN-10: 0-924047-54-2 (pbk. : alk. paper)
1. Blum, Liliana V., 1974---Translations into English. I. Kamei, Toshiya. II. Title.
PQ7298.12.L86A2 2008
863'.7--dc22
                              2008017281

Table of Contents

Acknowledgments

Stories from this collection have appeared in the following magazines:

Arkansas Literary Forum, The Bayou Review, Blackbird, The Dirty Goat, Eclectica, Farfelu, Hobart, Literal: Latin American Voices, Metamorphoses: A Journal of Literature & Art, Monkeybicycle, Mslexia, Pank, The Pedestal Magazine, Predicate, Spire, storySouth, Verbicide, Wanderings and *Words Without Borders.*

I would like to thank the following people who have made this book possible: Joe Bratcher, Tracey Hill and Anand Ramaswamy for entrusting me with this work, Gabriel Navar for lending us his artistic talent, Heidi Schmitt for gracing the cover, and Carolyn Walton for her generous financial support, which enabled me to complete this project.

– *Toshiya Kamei, 2008*

Translator's Note

The Curse of Eve is a first for both writer and translator – the first full-length short story collection for Liliana Blum, and my first book-length translation. And, at the risk of sounding patronizing, I like to think of Liliana V. Blum as my "discovery." When I first came across her work three years ago on the *Ficticia* website, her stories may not have seemed the obvious choice for a translator. She was not a member of Mexico City's literati, and her work had not been widely published. However, I was just starting out as a translator, and I wanted to work with a writer who was also at an early stage of her career.

An award-winning short story writer, Liliana Blum is one of the first Mexican writers of her generation to be translated into English. By her own admission, Blum's literary taste is *norteamericanizado*, and she counts among her influences such writers as Margaret Atwood, Barbara Gowdy and Bret Easton Ellis. However, unlike many internationally educated Mexican writers, she sets her fiction in her native country, more specifically Durango, her birthplace in arid northern Mexico. A few of her recent stories take place in Tampico, the hot and humid port on the Gulf of Mexico, but Blum returns again and again to Durango, where she spent the "most difficult years" of her life.

As many readers have noted, Blum's stories often conjure up a foreboding atmosphere, setting the stage for tragic events. Although her fiction contains lighthearted moments, she is drawn, like her literary influences, to the dark side of human nature. Dubbed by a male colleague a "damned feminist," Blum's fiction explores the lives of Mexican women from diverse backgrounds. Not surprisingly, many of these stories deal with violence against women, and with the restrictive roles imposed on wives and mothers.

In addition to my own literary taste, the author's gender played a role in my decision to translate her. I consciously choose to translate Latin American women writers, who are still underrepresented in literary magazines and anthologies published in their countries. It has been my privilege to work with Blum and her literary sisters, and I hope to continue giving them a voice in English.

— *Toshiya Kamei, 2008*

The Curse of Eve
and other stories

A New Faith

The fresh morning air frees all objects from their own weight. Peaches, oranges, apples and figs float upwards from the branches of the trees and the mossy ground. As you stand among the fruits, a flock of birds comes to you — owls, with their catlike eyes. Their wings cast a shadow across your mind, taking you to forbidden places. You fly over the vine-draped wall, leaving the garden and your beliefs behind. You find yourself naked, inevitably naked, without your dark habit and without shame. In your mind there is only the murmur of fluttering wings — and a peculiar pleasure. The owls caress you, hiding among your breasts and legs…

A bell tolls in the distance and the owls fly away clumsily. It's the time of the day when everything begins. You smell your damp fingers and you recognize what's inside: this is *you*. When you were a little girl, they told you there was a soul inside every person. You wonder if you have pieces of your soul smeared between your fingers.

The sisters prepare for the first prayers of the day. In silence, you too get ready in the darkness of the cell. The other nuns are already in the chapel. No one notices you arriving a few minutes late. You kneel down and close your eyes, anonymous among all those women who, like you, wear a habit. They're all chastity and devotion. Do they dream the same things you dream?

A lone owl flies inside you. *Go away*, you murmur to yourself. You try to concentrate, and pray to be strong. It's useless. You think this must be what eternity feels like. Time is a brown snail that climbs an endless mossy wall, halts to eat, then inches forward slowly. The chapel smells of fresh flowers. Your mouth moves mechanically, but you don't pray. The snail stops to rest. You wonder if it will ever reach the end of the wall. The chapel also smells of incense. The snail begins to move again. Incense and sad women, that's what this place smells of. You pretend to sing.

"Sister Paula" – someone taps you on the shoulder – "it's time to go." You look at no one as you head for the exit. The snail falls from the wall, leaving only the sticky trail of its journey. Its shell cracks on the cobbled floor.

*   *   *

There are no voices during breakfast – only the clinking of bowls as spoons go in search of a little more oatmeal; throats that open and close gulping liquids down; dentures and old age chewing without modesty. Breakfast mustn't be enjoyed, only thanked for. You swallow your food and look at your sisters in Christ. Is this really happiness? Did all of them decide to become nuns of their own free will? You wonder if they know about your past. It's supposed to be a secret – your mother made sure of that. "A good girl from a proper family can't turn out like this. What will people say?" You know it wasn't a question of being able to keep the baby or not: it was a simple problem of appearances. "What will people say?" your mother whined every day. Then the family doctor came and in silence did his work in you. Your mother's money made him forget. There is always enough money to make people forget anything. Your parents brought you to this convent when you were only fifteen: they told you this was your punishment for loving a man without permission from God or the law. Again and again your mother was guided by what others would say, and you never knew who they were – those *others* who could say the terrible things she was so afraid of.

In the convent no one talks during breakfast. You drink your coffee without sugar.

*   *   *

The high-ranking nuns think you have a gift with children. For years you have taught in the elementary school managed by the convent. Because you have great patience and the children adore you, your superiors don't think you need a teacher's certificate. You have an advantage over the other sisters who have to stay in the convent to cook and clean all day long. You consider yourself lucky. For you this is an escape, a window to the world, small sweets that brighten your day. But you find yourself imagining what your child would have been like, knowing that you'll never know. And with these thoughts, you're always overcome by the urge to cry. The children in your class try to console you, and you smile bitterly: "It's nothing. It's nothing." It's never nothing.

You examine each one of their drawings. The children had to sketch God as they imagined him. Most drew poor copies of the pictures in their catechism: a good-natured elderly man with sunbeams coming out of his divine head. But you see a drawing that catches your attention: an owl-like creature flying through a gray sky, with tears welling up in its large eyes. The next day you seek out the little artist. "Why is God crying?" you ask the girl, watching your own reflection in her large black eyes. "God cries because he has no friends and he has to be alone," she explains, with the resignation of an old monk. Then she starts playing nervously with her dark braids. You wait. "You can go now, Alejandrina." You give her drawing an A, of course. The girl goes away, skipping lightly, without stepping on the gray lines between the cobblestones.

*   *   *

You pause to read the black letters someone scribbled on the tomato you were about to put in your basket: *E tu, che cosa farai quando Dio è morto?* On your knees, you scan the garden to see if someone is watching you, but your eyes find only nuns mechanically picking vegetables. "*E tu, che cosa farai quando Dio è morto,*" you repeat to yourself, wondering who could have written it. The sun draws beads of sweat on your forehead. You need time to think. A cloud darkens the ground. You can feel the coolness of the passing shadow. Is it your flock of owls? It's a special moment, but the sunbeams have returned and you have to let your eyes readjust to the light. You hear dogs barking on the other side of the fence. Or is it a demon howling?

Making sure no one is watching you, you hide the tomato inside your sleeve and return to the convent with the excuse that you don't feel well. And you don't. When you rise to your feet, your step is shaky and your forehead burns. The fresh air in the corridor clears your head a little and you decide to throw away the tomato. It must be just the joke of some mischievous boy who escaped to play in the garden during the break. You tell the Mother Superior about your condition. Maternal, she feels your warm forehead and advises you to rest. "You have permission to miss the afternoon prayers," she says. When you arrive in your cell, you put the tomato on the bare nightstand, close your eyes, and give way to exhaustion. *And you, what will you do when God is dead?*

Death is gentle, bald, and rides a silver-colored horse. Each time she reaches at her destination, she dismounts from her horse and walks barefoot. Her long feet are covered with calluses, her coarse hands with warts. Always exhausted, always working. Her vulva is dry and dusty. Death is a refined lady with good manners. She dances naked, phantom breasts, under the sun. She acts as if she were the star of a circus that never ends. The lizards give her a big round of applause. Death goes through the audience with a feather hat, smiles with her pearly teeth, teeth of eternal marble. Death confesses she often gets bored with her job.

And in your dream you want to beg Death to take you with her. But she's gone.

Each time you crawl into bed, you long desperately, futilely, for your rapist. For a moment you tremble with emotion as you feel a hand, but it's Sister Catalina, who, obligingly, wipes your damp forehead. Other nuns gather around your bed and pray for you. Can you feel their prayers? Can they cure you of this sickness? Your eyes remain shut, the sweat trickles down between your breasts, but the nuns only daub your face. You don't notice, but Sister Catalina finds the tomato and takes it to the Mother Superior, along with your student's drawing of God, which you had hanging above your head. The sister crosses herself and leaves your cell in silence. The others follow her. A flock of owls returns to take you. And now it's true; the demons howl behind the walls of the convent.

The world was in darkness. The moon fell from the sky that day, and, without feet, she walked on a path of many colors. She had fallen from a height, but she never sprouted wings from her cratered shoulder blades. The moon began to walk the earth eternally. The dogs went mad. The elves stopped playing with the oranges in the tree. The tips of their ears pointed toward the moon. And they knew exactly what to do. Fugit irreparabile tempus...

For an hour you have been awake and have looked in vain for the tomato. A novitiate comes shyly into your cell and hands you a message. She leaves without looking you in the eye. You get dressed and in no time you find yourself knocking on the door of the Mother Superior's office. She is seated behind her large desk. She looks at you sternly, and, without a word, orders you to sit down. The room smells of pinewood and old portraits. The Mother Superior talks to you for a long time: the tomato, the drawing, the ever-existing doubts about your vocation, the devil's work in you, the punishments that befit you.

"Sister Paula, you can't continue teaching the children. You're a bad influence on them. From now on, as a punishment, your job will be cleaning Father Girasol's rooms." She keeps on talking, but you no longer listen. You bow humbly, as if you were truly contrite. But you can only think of your new duties. You feel like someone has opened an umbrella inside your stomach.

Hours later you inform Father Girasol that you'll be in charge of cleaning his small apartment. You try not to stare too intently at his hair, dark as eggplant, at his pear-shaped eyes and walnut-colored skin. You stop yourself before you imagine his figure under the dark forbidden cassock. "Then you must be the girl with the tomato," he jokes. You blush pink and dare to ask him how he knows it. "I know many things," he answers, smiling. He hands you the keys and tells you to clean when he's out. "I understand," you nod, obedient and wicked. You wonder if Father Girasol has noticed that your body is all smiles under your habit.

You turn the light off and the sun flares up automatically. The flock of owls stops flying and perches on a post, one owl on top of another like a feathered totem pole that watches you. A whole field of sunflowers turns their petalled heads toward you. You pour yourself a glass of milk to eat the breadcrumbs you have left on Father Girasol's brown body.

You're awake for a couple hours before the morning prayers. You leave your cell on tiptoe and go to the room upstairs, where the pigeons take refuge among the junk. Ignoring the stench that pierces your nose, and making your way through the feathers floating in the air, you arrive at the small wooden window with broken panes. In front of the convent the faint light of a streetlamp protects the pigeons and moths from the complete darkness. You watch a cat as it scurries across the street without looking and without any destination, a game of Russian roulette, a game of life.

At dawn the dogs start barking in the distance. Insomnia.

*   *   *

You have longed for this moment all day. Slowly, you open the door with the key he gave you. The fresh air from the lime wall caresses your skin. You feel as if you were in another world, far from the heat, the sisters, and everything else. The room smells of citrus fruit and the wet dirt of the plants Father Girasol surely watered before he left. You look around. It feels as if time has stopped. There are books everywhere and you can't stop smiling. Reading secular books is strictly forbidden in the convent and you have a great collection of them before you. There are books on the kitchen table, dishes waiting for the soap and scrubber, more books and clothes on the carpet, books everywhere, on the wicker chairs and on his desk. Books between the green sheets of his bed. You pick one up from the floor. The books are scattered as if they were breadcrumbs. Are you a Gretel who has to follow this path of books? Will you find a Hansel when you reach the end? *Of Love and Other Demons*. You didn't know García Márquez wrote this book. Then you realize you have been in the convent for a long time. But what does it matter anyway when you will spend the rest of your life locked up inside? Bitterly you leaf through the book.

With your eyes shut you imagine Father Girasol reading a few pages of this book and putting it down to pick up a different book. Is this what he does when he's not in the chapel? You imagine him lying on the sofa or rolling on the rug. You try to trace his movements, going from book to book, breathing in the fragrance of the pages. You try to identify a smell. You daydream about his aroma. You imagine his hair smells like mint, he has the scent of chocolate in his mouth, of tobacco on his hands, and his skin smells like oranges. You begin to read until your flock of owls comes for you.

You make love to him until you are both left drained. The sound of wings is always present. His skin is burning and though you have licked every inch of his body, even his eyes, he's still scorching. You fan him with huge lettuce leaves and dance for him. The moon has finally stopped walking. One of the lizards does a triple back somersault. You feel a small jolt of happiness surging from your dark, salty triangle and embedding itself in each vertebra.

You open your eyes very slowly, basking in the afterglow of orgasm. You'll feel different early tomorrow. For the moment, you hurry and clean the apartment. You feel so tired, as if you had made love to the writers of all the books you picked up and put on the bookshelf.

By the time you finish cleaning the sun has slipped away.

*   *   *

At night Mass, only your body fills a place in the third pew on the left. Your imagination runs free and you're afraid Father Girasol will notice that you hide under his black cassock, that you're building a new church, a new faith that stands on those two splendid pillars of muscle.

But the Mass ends and you have to go back to your chores. It's raining – everything is wet.

It's also raining outside in the garden.

*   *   *

As you expected, Father Girasol doesn't bat an eye at your confession. Because he knows he's so beautiful? You begin to suspect you're not the first one to confess her desire for the Father. He whispers the prayers of the rite of confession and you're forgiven immediately. "Forgiven for everything?" you ask. "Yes, Sister Paula. For everything." Then he tells you what your penance will be, but you don't listen. You don't want to be forgiven. You breathe intensely on the dark confessional curtain. You were right: Father Girasol smells like oranges. You kiss the air and leave.

*   *   *

The moon has walked thousands of miles since you first made love to Father Girasol's books and his image. The owls have shed their feathers many times since that day when you found him on his knees, writing quotes in different languages on cabbages, tomatoes, and squashes.

Now you find yourself each morning picking vegetables coded with messages he leaves for you. During Mass, the hours for meditation, and the meals, you close your eyes and pretend to pray while pulling the wings off small cupids. Then you go to that place – so secret and so obvious.

You haven't seen Death and her lizards since then. *And you, what will you do when God is dead?*

The Book Can
Still Be Mended

That cloudy afternoon, after spotting a couple of scorpions inside the saucepan for quince jelly, María de las Maravillas realized she would go blind. In sixty-five years her eyesight had never once failed her – but as her glance traveled to the scorpions' orange backs, she was so certain she would lose her eyesight that her limbs began to quiver and her back went numb, as if she had been fatally poisoned. She dropped the saucepan, and it rolled on its edge like a hula dancer's hips. The scorpions crawled into cracks in the wall behind the jars of peaches in syrup. She didn't try to kill the scorpions or scream for help. She didn't run away or try to understand. She just stood there. She couldn't have said how long she was there, whether it was a few minutes or a few hours. No one missed her, or rather everyone took her for granted. Twilight, the dark beetle crawling, began to bring in chunks of shadow through the pantry window. She smoothed her apron down and left. She wondered if Noah had felt the same emptiness inside when he learned about the upcoming flood. Or Lot, when the angels told him God would destroy his city. Revelations are always devastating. Not knowing the future is bliss.

It seemed much later, but the sound of the church bells reminded María de las Maravillas that it was almost seven. Soon her soap opera would come on, so she headed for the TV room. On the recliner, her husband was reading his third or fourth book of the week. In her case, it wasn't women or vices that snatched her husband's affection away from her, but literature. This silent lover not only kept her husband away from María, but also lived in the house, slowly overflowing the bookshelves. She thought his books would end up forcing them out of their home one day, as in a story she had made herself read many years ago in an attempt to please her husband, or rather to seduce him, following the advice she had read in a women's magazine. She'd heard him talking to a friend about a story by someone called Cortázar, and she'd had no problem finding it on the bookshelf, which was almost professionally ordered. Even though María de las Maravillas had read the story and tried to discuss the dark relationship between the characters, Don Buenaventura didn't appreciate her efforts. He didn't jump with joy. Nor did he become more attentive to her. His regard for her didn't increase. Instead, he told her that she was interrupting his reading. Besides, he added, that kind of book wasn't appropriate for women. *Find out his interests. Do research, learn, and have an intelligent conversation with him. This will make him want you more than ever. There's nothing quite like a smart brain to rekindle the flame in your marriage. Men prefer smart women.* That same afternoon María threw away the magazine along with the leftovers, and promised herself she'd never again follow someone else's advice to try and light up her marriage. It would be better if her marriage went up in flames once and for all so she could sweep the ashes under the rug.

"María, can you turn on the lamp?"

"I'm going blind."

"What?"

"I'm going blind."

"That's why I'm telling you to turn the light on, woman. It's already dark. I don't want to strain my eyes."

María de las Maravillas took several steps toward the corner, stomping her heels against the speckled floor. She pulled the chain on the standard lamp, within arm's reach of Don Buenaventura. He didn't take his eyes off the page. As always, she puffed and panted, flaring her nostrils like a bull about to charge. Long ago, this gesture would have made her husband realize she was annoyed, but now he didn't even raise an eyebrow. His ability to feel for her seemed to have eroded, like the stones that become blunt with the constant clash of waves.

"Didn't you hear me? Of course not, you never listen to me," she said, almost to herself. She sank into the couch, leaned her head back, and opened her eyes. At the upper corner of the wall, a shiny cobweb seemed to hold the entire weight of the old house. She looked up at the ceiling and noticed flecks of paint peeling off, like the skin of her knuckles after washing the sweat-stained collars of Buenaventura's shirts.

"Yes, I heard you. You're going blind. I'm not deaf yet. What you're telling me is old news. With the passage of time, you'll lose your senses, one by one, until you die. You're not discovering anything new, María."

"I thought you didn't hear me. Why didn't you answer me?"

"I heard you, but I have nothing to say. What's the point in worrying about the inevitable? Besides, I'm reading. I need light. And peace and quiet. I want you to stop interrupting me."

María de las Maravillas wanted to say that she would go blind very soon. Her mouth hung open for a few seconds, like a toad lying in wait for a dragonfly. Her intention vanished into thin air when she saw her husband immersed in the pages of his book.

A long-legged spider came sliding down from the cobweb. It crawled along the wall and disappeared behind Grandma Matilde's portrait – a sepia photo of a woman with a rigid back, a tight smile, cold eyes, a tense jaw, a frown like a fan. The photo captured not only the woman's image but also her unhappy life. María drew her brown shawl around her shoulders, rubbed her arms, and looked out the iron-barred window. Didn't her face look like her grandmother's? She watched the rain pour down, dragging with it the remains of garbage and memories, which would remain stuck in the sidewalk drains. The sky became tinged with dark purple, and she shivered. A flash of lightning illuminated her face, and the windows shuddered. For a second, her husband's figure became a silhouette. Almost muted, the soap opera flickered on the screen, like a dying glowworm.

"It's seven thirty," Don Buenaventura said, putting down his glasses and his book on the table. María got up in silence and headed for the kitchen. She heated the milk and placed bread, sugar, and instant coffee on the table. The chime of the grandfather clock confirmed the time. She looked at the clock and remembered it was a wedding gift from Grandma Matilde. A slight headache throbbed at her temples when she tried to remember the clock's age. She gave up and told her husband that everything was ready. They had snacks together and talked about nothing in particular, like any other evening for the last forty-five years. But that rainy day, María de las Maravillas knew, inexplicably but surely, that she would go blind.

*   *   *

It was still dark when the bells of San Agustín announced the six o'clock Mass. The sexton was sweeping the courtyard, shuffling orange peels, gnawed-up corncobs, cigarette butts, and other garbage that the faithful, in their fervor and devotion, forgot to put in the trashcans. The broom raised a cloud of dust, which flew for a few moments and landed on the ground like a flock of homeless pigeons. Outside, on the sidewalk and in the lay world, the view was even worse. Besides the usual litter, the stink of urine floated up from the wall near the sacred ground. A bucket of water with chlorine and a brush would have taken care of the problem, but that was where the sexton's responsibility ended and City Hall's duties began: the iron gate drew a line between what belonged to God and what belonged to Caesar. The chubby man with the onion-shaped body did no more than shove a pile of garbage toward the sidewalk. He crossed himself before going back inside as the service was about to start.

The old women who covered their heads with dark shawls, salt and pepper, and blind faith gathered inside the church. They moved their lips, asking their favorite saints for love, health, money, and miracles, and promising in return to make a few small sacrifices. A pair of bleary-eyed altar boys set out the instruments of rite and poured water over fresh chrysanthemums on both sides of the altar. With her chin buried in her collarbone, María de las Maravillas prayed in silence. Even though she pretended to join in the songs and prayers and listen to the sermon during the Mass, she never stopped talking to her personal God. The smell of incense, fresh flowers, and old people who bathed only once a week mixed with the congregation's out-of-tune voices joining in the morning prayer.

In the confessional, María de las Maravillas hesitated in front of the dark curtain that shielded her from Father Girasol's sour breath. Just as she opened her mouth to confess, she decided not to mention the revelation she'd had the previous afternoon. Instead, she rattled off her harmless sins and correctly guessed her penitence. She blocked out the priest's voice and thought about leaving the church and walking around the city, seeing everything for the last time. She left the confessional without excusing herself. For several hours, she walked through the old district, which she had known as a girl, trying to engrave everything she saw on her mind. That morning she realized she could survive in the shadows.

*   *   *

María de las Maravillas decided that once she lost her sight, she wouldn't leave her home again. She was determined to use whatever time she had left to learn to live without her eyesight. She spent all her energy, all her sadness, all her time trying to commit to memory every detail of the house.

Salomón, her cat, began to miss the warm afternoons spent on María's lap while she knitted. Don Buenaventura missed his wife's presence on the couch next to him. They didn't talk to each other, but she was always a part of the furniture. It felt as if someone had redecorated the room and it bothered him. Lately María de las Maravillas did nothing but walk around the house blindfolded. She would stop a million times in the hallways and touch every inch of the walls, of the bookshelves, of the doors, and of any object she found. She even stopped going to the afternoon Mass and attended only the morning service. She said she wouldn't make quince jelly or peaches in syrup or cakes until she felt sure she could do it without seeing. When her soap opera came on, she would sit down in her usual place, still blindfolded, and listen to the dialogue coming from the screen, imagining what the characters were doing. This particularly annoyed her husband, but the worst was when she tried to serve snacks, feeling her way, spilling milk and instant coffee grounds on the tablecloth. He complained, but María said he had to get used to it because everything would change once she became blind. Don Buenaventura, who hated marital quarrels, chose to overlook his "blind" wife's blunders.

*   *   *

After practicing the art of blindness for almost a year, María de las Maravillas came to know even the remotest part of her house. She acquired the skills to make marmalade, preserve fruits, and even bake cookies. She managed the kitchen like the world's best cook. She could make the beds, do the dishes, dry them, and put them in their places. She could wash clothes, iron them, and even mend them with her eyes closed.

One afternoon, María de las Maravillas was looking in the pantry for a sack of beans. She suddenly stopped as if an unfamiliar voice warned her of danger. Disconcerted, but curious, she slowly removed her blindfold and pulled the chain above her head to turn on the light. After her eyes adjusted to the brightness, she saw a large yellow scorpion near the sack. She didn't need her eyes to dodge this danger: that day she knew she was ready to live without her eyesight. She stomped on the poor creature and left the pantry to shower kisses on Don Buenaventura's bald head. She told him they would celebrate with hot chocolate and a fresh-baked apple pie.

*   *   *

The next morning, María de las Maravillas got up at five, as usual, to attend the first Mass of the day. She strode through the darkness, her bare feet touching the floor. She finished fixing herself up and still had half an hour before the bells of San Agustín began to toll. She decided to sit down and work on the sweater she was knitting for her favorite grandson. When she thought it was time to go, she stepped forward, carrying her yarn and knitting needles to put inside the basket in the corner of the room. She wasn't blindfolded, but walked with her eyes closed. Just as she rested her weight on her right leg, she tripped and lost her balance. She fell flat on her face, an intense breeze caressing her face for a fraction of a second. For the last time, she saw the white wall, the yellow yarn, the silvery knitting needles. Then everything went dark.

Don Buenaventura left his room, grumbling. He'd had too much pie the day before and had heartburn. A muffled cry and a dull thud on the floor had woken him. He went into the TV room. His wife lay on the floor, the knitting needle piercing her right eye. Beside her body, a book with shiny pages lay open, slightly damaged. "I must've dropped it last night when I fell asleep," he thought. He hesitated for a few seconds. He picked up the book and decided to try to glue the torn pages together. "Maybe it can still be mended."

Bride Wanted

Gabriel turned off the engine a few yards away from the house and tiptoed to the main entrance. His mother always left the door unlocked during the day, and he easily popped it open. When he walked into the living room, his mother and her friend choked on their coffee and the cups clinked loudly in their saucers. Their hands were shaking. The two old women had lifted their flabby hips as if caught fornicating. Of course they were talking about him. What else would they talk about? Stupid old hags, they couldn't even pretend to be chatting about something else. He loved his mother, but he couldn't stand seeing her with that gossipy woman, who was putting ideas into her head. Doña Socorro quickly wiped her mouth.

"Gabito, I wasn't expecting you back so soon."

Gabriel walked past them, leaving footmarks on the worn

carpet. He disappeared through the hallway and shut himself in his room.

Doña Socorro gave an embarrassed smile, the kind that leaves many a wrinkle on mothers' faces. She smoothed her skirt and tried to make the best of the situation. "Did I tell you we're going to place a personal ad in the local paper?"

"What for?"

"To find Gabito a good wife."

"A wife?"

Doña Carmelita had met Socorro when they were visiting their respective sons in prison. Her son was locked up for taking seeds and fertilizers from his boss's warehouse and selling them at cost; Soco's son was in for corruption of minors. In the end, after so many visits together, they became friends. Everyone had given Socorro the cold shoulder when they heard about Gabriel's arrest. But Socorro wasn't a bad person. She was selfless and hard working, and, like all mothers of prisoners, she had never stopped believing in her son. But there are different kinds of crimes. Carmelita was terrified of Gabriel, but she still visited her friend out of Christian love, to comfort the lonely woman.

"Yes, a good wife," Doña Socorro said, as if she were offended. Then she relaxed a bit. "I'm not always going to be here to look after him, Carmen. What will become of him when I'm gone? You know about my diabetes."

Señora Carmelita nodded, sucked her lower lip between her teeth, and opened her eyes wide. She didn't want to say that Gabriel was over thirty, or mention the sexual perversion that had put him in prison in the first place. If Socorro thought her son was innocent, it wasn't Carmen's job to make her see the light. Friends support each other.

Socorro took out a small, folded piece of paper from her apron pocket and began to smooth it out as she adjusted her glasses. "I'm going to read you what I wrote. Let me know what you think, okay?"

Carmen nodded and gulped down her coffee. The coffee Socorro served was almost always lukewarm from the start. She tried to sit up, but only sank back into the couch.

"Young, good-looking male seeking female aged 25-35 for serious relationship and marriage."

"You need to say more about him. His likes and dislikes, if he smokes or not, things like that."

"I was thinking those other things come later, when they get to know each other, you know, when they go out a few times."

"Soco, if I were a young girl looking through the personal ads, I wouldn't answer this one."

"You wouldn't? Then what should I say?"

Carmen opened her mouth, but nothing came out. She felt someone standing behind her. She wouldn't be surprised if Gabriel were getting ready to stab them right at that very moment. Showing no sign of fear, she pretended to drink from her empty cup and tried to meet Socorro's eyes. But her friend was looking down at the piece of paper in her hands.

"How about 'A pedophile, a convicted rapist who lives with his mother and enjoys walking in the park to spy on the kids and surfing the Internet for porn'?" Gabriel was leaning against the wall, his arms crossed over his chest. He watched the two women and sneered as if he had a cigarette hanging out of his mouth. His eyes were deep and expressionless. His cold glance made Carmen's hairs stand on end.

"Honesty is important in relationships, Ma. We don't want to deceive anyone."

Carmelita cleared her throat, wiped her lips, and left a napkin smeared with coffee and red lipstick on the table. As she pulled her body out of the couch, she tried to focus on the painting of cherubs that hung on the wall. She didn't want to meet Gabriel's eyes. It terrified her that he mocked his own sexual deviations, his filthy sins, as if he were proud of them. How could he enjoy humiliating his own mother? Was nothing sacred to this monster? May God curse him, she thought. I don't ever want to meet him in heaven.

"Socorrito, I'll see you tomorrow at Mass."

"Yes, Carmelita. Thank you for coming."

As soon as Gabriel disappeared into the kitchen, Socorro murmured, "Please excuse him. He's not well. They've told him he's guilty so many times that he now believes it himself. This is how he shows his frustration – that's what his psychologist told us."

Señora Carmen took a deep breath and walked slowly toward the door. There was no use in talking about the same thing all over again. Socorro had many virtues, but the ability to recognize her son's mistakes was not one of them.

"You know I've put him on my group's prayer list. Don't worry, Soco. He'll change. He'll change." Carmen tried to force a smile, but the muscles in her face were too stiff. She was in a hurry to leave.

"Yes, thank you so much. I'm glad you came."

*　　*　　*

In the kitchen Gabriel was dipping a piece of ginger bread into his cup of milk.

"What are you going to cook for my snack, Ma?"

"Nothing. I'm upset with you."

"Your friend, that fat cow, is too sensitive. She's not used to assertiveness. You should take her to my madhouse nurse."

"She's not a madhouse nurse, Gabriel. She's a psychologist. Don't make fun of her. She said you were getting much better."

"Sure. I know how to behave in front of her, I tell her what she wants to hear. I just want her to shut up. I can't stand her voice."

"No, she told me you've improved a lot. She said you'd be fine."

"I'm as normal as any pervert on the street, Ma. The difference is that I got caught."

"*Mijito*, every time you say that, it hurts me here." Doña Socorro touched her chest, between her sagging breasts. "The doctor was the one who suggested we find you a wife."

"Maybe you should take Pepto Bismol. I'm not a dog, so don't go looking for a bitch for me."

Doña Socorro collapsed on the chair. She poured herself a cup of milk, added two spoonfuls of coffee crystals, and stared into the creamy spiral.

"Gabriel, please. Do it for me. You know I'm not going to last very long. It'll make me happy if we put the ad in the paper and you go out with a woman. Then I can die in peace. Listen to me, Gabito."

"Ma, you're not going to die anytime soon."

"I haven't told you this, but my last checkup didn't turn out so good. All these worries have made my diabetes worse. And you know I have high blood pressure. Let's put the ad in the paper, okay? Promise me you'll go out with someone who answers, Gabriel. Come on, *mijo*. When I'm dead, I can't bother you anymore."

"Okay, fine, Ma. But I'm only doing this because you want me to." Gabriel swallowed his bread and wiped his forearm across his mouth. "I'm going online for a while. Could you bring me some quesadillas?"

"Oh, Gabo. Thank you. When Carmelita comes tomorrow, I'm going to place the ad in the paper."

*   *   *

After the personal ad appeared in the paper, Doña Socorro received four phone calls. She answered each call and then handed the receiver to her son so he could set up a date with the potential bride. Each time he chose to meet the girl at a bench in front of the duck pond in Guadiana Park. From Tuesday to Friday, her son had a date every day, Doña Socorro told her friend. She could hardly believe it – it was just wonderful.

But things didn't turn out as she had hoped. That Friday, when Carmelita came to visit Socorro, she saw tears in her friend's eyes and found a bottle of *rompope* on the table. Socorro served Carmen some *rompope* right away, then poured some for herself, and gave her a sad look. The first three dates had been disaster, according to Gabriel. What had happened? asked Carmen. Socorro started to retell Gabriel's story between sighs and sniffles. She suppressed a cry, her eyes welling up.

The woman he met on Tuesday was a hippo. Her son didn't even want to talk to her – he just abandoned her in the middle of the park. Doña Soco hated to imagine what rude words he had said to the poor girl. His date on Wednesday was a fiasco too. The woman, a successful accountant, was in her forties, wore elegant clothes, and drove a luxurious car. Maybe that's why he had deigned to ask her a bit about her life and even accepted her invitation to dine at a fine restaurant. But after the dinner, Gabriel told her she was too old for him, that he already had a mother. Can you believe it, Carmelita?

Carmen drank up her *rompope* and Socorro filled her cup again. Carmen thought what her friend had just told her was terrible. What had happened to the third woman? The third one was young, Soco answered, but she had a huge birthmark covering much of her face. Of course, Gabriel didn't even want to share the bench with her. God knows what cutting words he had hurled at the poor woman. He could be so cruel sometimes. Every afternoon he had come home and complained about his date. Wasn't going out with those monsters enough to prove his love for his mother? Then Gabriel would shut himself in his room and turn on the computer. Because he was surfing the Internet, Socorro couldn't use the phone until he finished. She sighed. At that moment Gabriel was in the park with his fourth date. Her last hope. She prayed this one would be different.

Carmelita tried her best to smile and kept herself busy picking lint off her skirt. Doña Socorro was visibly upset. From time to time she gave in to a fit of tears and then felt the need to justify herself. "Oh, Carmelita. Only you can understand – it breaks your heart to see your son behind bars. He's still your child, it doesn't matter what he's done. Now he's out of prison, but he can't rebuild his life. I can't stop loving him. What can I do? It doesn't matter what he has done – he's still my son. He came out of my womb. Carmelita, you understand me, don't you? The bond between mother and son is very strong. I want to die in peace."

"Calm down, Socorro. You'll see, your son will find a good wife. If not the first three times, maybe the fourth time will be a charm. You shouldn't lose hope."

Doña Socorro embraced her friend and sobbed for a while. Her tears wet Carmelita's sweater. Carmelita slowly untangled herself from Socorro's grasp.

"Remember, there are other women in town. Those four aren't the only ones, Soco."

A bit drunk, Carmelita left Socorro asleep on the couch and went home, taking the empty bottle of *rompope* with her.

*   *   *

The next day, Doña Socorro waited impatiently for her son to join her in the kitchen. She wrung her hands as if squeezing a rag. When Gabriel sat at the table, his mother hurried to serve him freshly squeezed orange juice. He sipped from his glass.

"How did it go?" she asked.

"I'm going to see her again tomorrow, Ma."

"Really, Gabriel?"

"Yes. Her name is Claudia. She's the oldest of five kids. Her mother died recently, and she lives with her dad. She's eighteen and studying to be a secretary. She looks after her younger siblings. Will you cook me an egg and chorizo?"

Tears trickled down her wrinkled face. She threw her arms around her son's neck and showered him with wet kisses.

"Oh, *mijito*. You don't know how happy I am. Be good to her, Gabriel. Behave yourself, be a gentleman."

Gabriel freed himself from his mother's arms, soft and sticky like jellyfish, and kissed her creased forehead. Of course he'll be a gentleman. She doesn't need to worry. Everything will be different this time. Placing a personal ad was a great idea. He's not going to miss this chance.

As Socorro began to fry the chorizo, the aroma filled the kitchen. Gabriel smiled, something he hadn't done in a long time.

Better Halves

As he inserted the key in the lock, turned the doorknob, and went into the house, all his doubts melted away. The fantasy had floated in his mind for many years, waiting for a sign, any pretext, to turn it into reality. If someone had asked him then, he couldn't have explained why he had the feeling that his life was about to take a dramatic turn, a sudden shift that would change things forever. Nor could he tell whether this certainty scared or excited him, or both.

The creak of the door gave away his presence. Just before he went inside, he heard his wife's frantic footsteps – the pat-pat of her slippers going down the stairs. There she was, with her curlers and her blue face-pack, like something out of a TV show. Under any other circumstance, this sight would have struck him as comical, but not tonight. He forced a smile, but, as usual, she put her hands on her hips – making her look like a plump jug – and started interrogating him. Irritated, she demanded to know why he had come home so late. What had he done since he left his office? Where the hell had he been? He tried to remain calm and explained that his workload had recently doubled, but before he knew it, he was being showered with bitter reproaches. His better half, beside herself with rage, was like a desert scorpion in a sealed jar. He knew he wouldn't get out unscathed if he tried to explain himself, so he kept his mouth shut, replaying last Saturday's soccer game in his mind. His wife began to throw plates at him from the kitchen, and as he dodged her missiles, he grew more and more exasperated.

At any other time, a quarrel with his wife would have made him feel guilty and bitter. He would have caressed her shoulder softly while she slept, her back against him – still dreaming that her husband was cheating on her. He would have made a half-hearted apology in hopes of avoiding the silent treatment she would give him the next day. But that night he slept like a baby. When he woke up in the morning, he found his wife gone. He didn't even wonder where she was. He calmly got dressed and went to work, convinced that he was going through something different for the first time in almost ten years.

Through the office window the fresh-looking city came into view, something unusual in those summer months in Tampico. He worked without distraction, as if last night's incident had never happened, and managed to finish most of his tasks. When the cathedral bells tolled four blocks from the building where he worked, he threw several documents into his briefcase, put on his sunglasses, and left, saying goodbye to his secretary, who looked at him suspiciously.

He dodged the pedestrians who zigzagged down the sidewalk like blind bats, stopping often to avoid a head-on collision. He wanted to walk in silence and reflect on what he was about to do.

But he could only think of trivial things like car maintenance and tax payments. It was his mind's trick – or was it his conscience's? – that blocked out what he had already decided.

A few minutes later, the red wooden door was flung open. A woman, whose best years, if she had any, had long gone, received him with a sullen smile. With sour manners that seemed carefully cultivated, she gestured for him to take a seat in the small waiting room. While he waited, he looked around. Outside, the neon sign crackled on and off, its sounds merging with female voices from the rooms and hallway. Inside, the blue velvet-covered furniture, large glass lamps that hung from the ceiling, golden ornaments on the papered walls, and worn red carpet seemed to insist on recreating an era that had never existed in the city. Even though the air conditioner purred, a stream of sweat trickled down his nervous back. The large grandfather clock, pretentious and out of date like the rest of the room, slowly ticked off the minutes.

He didn't know it, but just as he sat on the worn bed next to the young woman who stared at him with frightened eyes, and took her hand in his to try and reassure her, his wife had sworn in front of her best friend – over cappuccino and a slice of pecan pie – that she would make her husband wish he'd never been born, and that she would never give him a divorce. It was something he would find out later, when his daily life resumed. Without much thought, he threw himself into the arms of an unknown pleasure.

That night, like all brown cats in the port, he wandered the city streets, trying to feel remorse he couldn't feel – would never feel – even though he would taste pleasure many times more.

God Bless Ron Jeremy

"Even we nuns need a break sometimes." She leans over the table and steals a cigarette out of my pack. "Don't you smoke Viceroy anymore?"

"Nobody smokes Viceroy these days. Have you seen an ad for Viceroy recently?"

"We don't have TV in the convent."

I take one for myself and light hers. As a busty waitress refills our coffee cups, I watch Amaranta. Oblivious to the waitress's cleavage, she glances around the restaurant. From the exterior hallway of the second floor, which has been turned into a balcony with tables, you can see the kiosk that was once the patio of the house.

"Did you know this used to be the Durán Inn?" I ask.

"What?"

"The Durán family used to own this guesthouse. Then it became an expensive but mediocre hotel, and now it's a Sanborns."

Amaranta rolls back her eyes until the whites show. I remember how much this gesture would turn me on, her green eyes disappearing for a few seconds. We go a long way back. Fifteen, twenty years? Anyway, I was the first man in her life, and the one who broke her heart. Why, when I have nothing to say, do I start sounding like a tour guide?

I smoke because I don't know what else to say. I smoke because today was supposed to be like any other day. As always, I was going to drink coffee and read the paper before going to my office. Why did she have to be at the table next to mine? Why did she have to recognize me? Why did she have to come over to my table with her coffee and bread and keep me company? As an awkward silence grows between us, the spoons clink against the cups, hurting my ears. I have a headache.

"Why did your parents choose your name, Amaranta?"

She pours cream into her coffee. Several drops splash on my shirt cuffs.

"People always ask me that question. I should curse my parents for this." She stirs her coffee vigorously, splashing some over the edge of her cup. She pouts like a little girl. "But I can't. You know, the Commandments. Honor your father, blah blah blah."

I only manage a grimace. I don't feel like talking. I don't want to be here. Nor do I want to remember Amaranta when she was young, when she still had smooth skin, and hopes. She was never beautiful, but she moved with the urgency of an old maid making up for lost years. Our affair was a pragmatic arrangement. Amaranta seemed to have a talent for straddling my body, dashing straight toward her orgasms. She was a natural-born slut. Or maybe, knowing she wasn't young anymore, she wanted to make the best use of what she had. Maybe she loved me. I don't know.

"My mother, 'the well-read person'" – Amaranta makes quotation marks in the air with her fingers – "was reading *One Hundred Years of Solitude* when she was pregnant with me." She slugs down her coffee and winks at me. "She must have misplaced *Good Housekeeping* and *Cosmo*. She didn't have anything else to read in the bathroom."

I'm obliged to keep a respectful silence as Amaranta mentions her mother's bodily functions. My mind flashes back to her mother's image: an attractive mature lady who looked a full ten years younger than her real age. Always wearing makeup, thin, a queen of the Palacio de Hierro department store. It was one of those rare cases where the mother is much more beautiful than the daughter. Her father's bad genes had ruined everything for Amaranta.

"Pregnant women are always constipated. That's the only explanation – she wouldn't have finished the book otherwise." Amaranta laughs and flashes the same smile, the one she would use to ask, "Are you ready now?" before she mounted me again. Getting hard wasn't a problem for me back then. I was like the Duracell Bunny when it came to fornication. We used each other again and again until we were both drained. I look at her. Do I look so old? She squeezes the cigarette butt as if it were a small accordion.

"So, there you go – they named me after Amaranta Buendía."

"Oh dear." I feel like an idiot. What can I say to this woman? She may have been mine once, but it's so long ago that it seems like someone else's experience. Taking my silence for approval, she goes on with her story.

"Parents, my dear Pablo, have their own way of screwing up your life." She takes another Marlboro, without asking. She still behaves as if she owns the world. That was one of the reasons I broke up with her – that, and her countless selfish orgasms. Or maybe it was the way she made me feel used? Or the fact that I liked someone else? I don't really remember.

"Now I go by Sister Purificación. The girls at the convent school call me Mother Pura."

"And why did you...?"

Amaranta, forty-something, with short hair, without earrings, no makeup to hide her wrinkles, white blouse, vest, brown skirt. Thick, white pantyhose, grandmotherish flat shoes. A cigarette between her fingers and a retired whore's expression on her face.

"You've been doing great. I read about you in the paper the other day. The Historical Association?"

I nod uncomfortably and order a few *sopecitos* for us. "At least I found a use for my trivial knowledge."

"I, on the other hand, found God." Amaranta combs her fingers through her hair, as if the sensation of her hair were the best thing in the world. I almost give in to the urge to touch her graying hair.

"It's nice to see you again. I thought I'd never see you again after that day."

"I always get something to drink here before I go to my office. It's just around the corner."

That day. She means the day we broke up. I don't know where Amaranta got the idea that I was going to marry her. I think women want marriage like squirrels want walnuts. I wasn't ready to settle down – with her or anyone else, but certainly not with her. I wanted to marry someone beautiful, a girl from a good family. Maybe I thought that would guarantee happiness. Maybe I didn't. It was a long time ago. How am I supposed to remember that far back?

"If I had to choose someone to share my life with, you would have been my first choice." Amaranta traces the edge of her empty cup with the tip of her finger.

I keep quiet. I'd rather be somewhere else. I'm not going to talk about my marriage, much less my divorce. I'm still licking my wounds.

"I saw the photos in the papers when you got married. Beautiful bride." Amaranta folds a *sope* in half and swallows it.

I notice no change in her voice, but I suspect she knows the whole story. The walls of convents aren't like they used to be, I suppose.

"So, how did you end up in the convent?"

"Thanks to Ron Jeremy."

"Excuse me?"

"Thanks to him I learned that my true calling was to seclude myself with the nuns of the Mariana congregation. I'll tell you if you like, but let's walk, shall we?"

I ask for the check. Of course I pay for both of us and Amaranta doesn't say anything. We go outside and the Veinte de Noviembre noises are all around us. My headache gets worse. I feel as if someone were covering and uncovering my ears with his hands. A dusty wind forces us to turn and start walking uphill. I wouldn't be surprised if I saw a roadrunner trailing after a tumbleweed.

"Years ago Ron Jeremy came to Durango to make two movies."

"Two?" The weather is ridiculous, like everything else today. It's cold when we walk in the shade, and when we walk in the light it's unbearably hot.

"You know, to make the best use of the trip. Two cowboy movies."

"No, I didn't know."

"Really? It was a huge scandal. The PTAs and Bible-thumpers made a big deal out of it. You must have heard about it."

"Maybe it was when I was working in Spain."

"I was still living with my parents. An only daughter, aging parents, the usual story."

"What sort of work were you doing?"

"I was working at the Golden Scorpion, a mini supermarket. We were doing well."

We walk past the cathedral. I cross myself clumsily out of habit. Amaranta laughs.

"Weren't you going to tell me about Ron Jeremy?"

Amaranta's step is light, too quick for a woman, especially for a woman her age. I always had to wait for my ex-wife. We stop at Bruno Martínez to cross the street. When we pass the Teatro Ricardo Castro, she picks up where she left off.

"Ron Jeremy came to shoot *Dancing with Bitches V* and *The Pimp, the Whore, and the Ugly*."

I look down and nod. I'm so fat I can hardly see the tips of my shoes. I keep my hands in my pant pockets. My bald head begins to sweat. I'm painfully aware of how pathetic I look.

"They were Western movies. You know. Nobody came to Durango to make any other type of movie. Anyway, I learned that Ron Jeremy was here. I showed up on the set. They were shooting at the Rancho La Joya."

"I know where that is. John Wayne used to own it."

"Yes. The place was totally in ruins, but you don't need a perfect set for that kind of movie. Anyway, I showed up. And I wasn't the only one – there was a line of idiots who all thought they'd get to go to bed with porn actresses. They were going to offer themselves as messenger boys or whatever. Men can be so gullible."

We start going up Calvario. Out of breath, Amaranta breaks off her story. But as soon as the path leads downhill again, she continues.

"Of course, they got kicked out. Anyway, they would have felt less than a man if they had seen Ron Jeremy in his entirety."

"Really?"

"You have no idea. When all the locals were gone, I walked in. I sold the actors soft drinks and snacks. I lined my pockets."

We wait for the traffic light on Dolores del Río Boulevard. Why did we come here? I let Amaranta bring me here.

"Where are we going?"

"Then I saw him. He was naked except for a towel around his waist. He had long hair, but he wasn't fat yet. He came over and said hello to me. He was such a gentleman."

Amaranta laughs again. She tells me how Ron talked to her between takes, how they hit it off and made a date for the next day. She showed him around the city; he showed her what he was famous for. They never saw each other again.

Before I realize it, we're in front of the entrance to Guadiana Park – the park where we would meet before we went to my house, the motel, anywhere we could go. The same place where I told her it was over between us. The place where I left her crying and walked away, feeling nothing. I look at my watch. It's almost one in the afternoon. I think about my car in the Madero Parking Lot, far away from here, too far to go back on foot.

"You have to go?"

"I've got stuff to do at the office."

"I have to go to one o'clock Mass at Los Ángeles. We're going to offer flowers to the Virgin."

"You never told me why you took the veil, Amaranta – you just told me your biggest erotic adventure."

"I thought you could figure it out yourself."

"Well, no. I'm afraid I don't understand you."

"After Ron Jeremy, I couldn't be with anyone else. It would be cruel to him, unfair on me. And then the Holy Spirit called me. Marriage wasn't for me."

"Oh." I don't know what else to say, but I want to get away from her as quickly as possible. This was going to be like any other day.

"God bless Ron Jeremy. It was all thanks to him that I found my path. Excuse me, Pablo. I'm running late for Mass. It was nice to see you."

She turns and crosses the street. I watch her until she disappears into the church, and then I flag down a cab. I've lived here all my life; I've never worked in Spain, or anywhere else – that's why I know Ron Jeremy has never been to Durango. But as they say, the truth is overrated.

The Debutante

Muffled footsteps echo in the carpeted hallway and stop suddenly in front of her door. The only sound comes from the neon sign, buzzing in the dark like flies stuck in a trap of light. Delfina feels the sweat trickling down her forehead and down her back. Her heart begins to beat rapidly. Her eyes search the shadows of the room for something familiar, something that could calm her. But everything seems distant and unknown. Her breath comes in sharp spasms, the air stuttering into her lungs. The door opens suddenly and he appears.

On the streets of downtown, the afternoon air becomes humid and sticky: a jellyfish of fire envelops the city and devours all the fresh air. The old buildings stand as witnesses to all that happens around them, and to what goes on within their walls; they are as worn as the clothes of the man who sweeps the sidewalks, futilely shuffling the dust and garbage from one place to another. Under their portals, aged prostitutes lazily flaunt themselves, their desires as decrepit as the gates of the old hotels. Like a lobster in a tank full of crayfish, *La Casa de Naná* stands out among all the old buildings. The façade is clean, recently painted, and without graffiti. The neon sign, stylish and attractive, has blue cursive letters. Inside, the air conditioner conceals the stifling heat of the port. The walls, covered in dark wood veneer, the red carpet, and the ornate golden lamps hanging from the ceiling clumsily imitate a nineteenth-century French brothel.

Delfina feels that the man is disappointed in her. She contemplates her own face, deathly pale, her eyes desolate and afraid. Her hands are visibly shaking. The man remains still, almost frozen at the threshold of the door. For a very long moment, she remembers her mother's constant screams, telling her she was good for nothing, a burden, a useless girl, a hussy who would never amount to anything – the bitter color of her childhood. Now she thinks that her mother's prophecies have come true: *you don't even deserve to be a good whore, Delfina*, she says to herself, without daring to raise her eyes.

The pigeons gather fiercely around the plaza, a swarm of locusts with gray and brown feathers, destroyers of the old cantera stone buildings. There are the city pigeons, enemies of the balloon sellers, who manage to live off the children who feed them; devout pigeons, more regular churchgoers than even the most ardent of Catholics; bomber pigeons, imminent danger on the electricity lines; therapeutic pigeons, a pastime for the elderly who spend their days throwing breadcrumbs on the ground; playful pigeons, who dart erratically from spot to spot, to the delight of small children; ideological pigeons, a symbol of peace; roasted pigeons, the food for the poorest of the poor...

"Get up and let me look at you," he orders, a hint of tenderness in his deep voice. Delfina rises slowly. She tries to calm her nerves, hiding the terror she feels inside. She stands in front of the man, displaying herself in the outfit the madam chose for her first night: a blouse unbuttoned to the level of her nipples, her firm round breasts, like opposing parentheses, revealing her young smooth curves; a black leather miniskirt that wraps around her flat belly and soft hips; dark pantyhose; and shiny high heels that make her teeter and threaten to knock her off her feet at any moment.

"Come here," the client orders, waving her to sit beside him on the bed. She moves as if in a dream, the blood pounding against her temples with a dull hissing sound.

"Don't be afraid. They already told me you haven't done this kind of work before. But there's nothing to be scared of, I'm just an ordinary guy. You look as if it were your first time!" he says, wrapping his arm around Delfina's shoulders.

"It *is* going to be my first time."

"Really? Well, I'm damned. I wasn't expecting this."

"Isn't that what all men want? A virgin?" she asks, barely audible.

"Well, for some men it's very important, I won't deny it. But that doesn't interest me."

Delfina remains quiet. A dark silence fills the room for a moment. The man clears his throat and loosens his tie.

"What's your name?"

"Roxana," she falters, fearing he can see through her lie. "And you?"

"I'm Juan... Juan Hernández," he lies, knowing it doesn't matter, that it's just the game everyone plays. "Look, Roxana. I'll tell you something. This is the first time I've come to a brothel to see a girl like you. I'm married, you know. And this is the first time... well, I've never cheated on my wife before."

Delfina looks up at her client and realizes he's not the repulsive monster she'd expected: he has a calm face and minty breath. When he kisses her, his lips are warm, and he embraces her softly, a stout torso in a clean shirt. She breathes deeply and feels unexpectedly relaxed. The masculine scent of his lotion fills her senses.

A round chalk-white moon is mirrored on the dark water that barely stirs with the splash of a few flying fish. The seagulls are asleep in the empty boats, their nests hidden in the thick ropes of the moorings. On the streets of the city, huge moths, driven mad by light, are hurling themselves against the streetlamps. Some adventurous crabs have abandoned the wharves to walk along the sidewalks, close to the wall, avoiding the pedestrians. The nightlife enjoys its prime and the hours pass quickly. In no time the drunks who have finished their reveling and the early risers on their way to work will mix with each other in the ambiguous hours of the morning. The prostitutes who work at night go to their rooms to rest. The waitresses hurry to arrange the chairs and prepare the coffee. The carved mahogany door of *La Casa de Naná* swings back and forth, spitting out gray, fading men who melt into the morning light. On the streets, there is only garbage, memories, empty cans, unfulfilled desires, vomit, urine, and broken promises.

The city wakes up slowly. Delfina, with rings under her eyes, starving, dressed in jeans and a T-shirt, wants to sleep deeply until the afternoon. With her hair in a ponytail and her face washed, she could easily pass for a high school student. But she knows her school days and the promise of improving herself are over. In her home, the need is great while the means are scarce. When she returns to her family, no one will congratulate her, nor will there be any reward for having finished her first day of work – the first day of the rest of her life. Her mother, bloated with regrets, will want to ask her, while filtering her sweet-smelling coffee, how much money she managed to earn. Her father will sink back into his chair, into a bad mood, hating himself. But no one in the family will say a word.

Delfina goes into the kitchen without saying hello. She grabs a piece of bread and pours herself a glass of milk. She just wants to fall into bed and go to sleep. She is haunted by the muffled silence of her pain, which, like the pigeons in the plaza, will become a part of her life.

Requiem for a Cherub

His mother always called him "cherub," showering kisses on his chubby, rosy cheeks, and spoiling him with all kinds of sweets. His father called him *little prick* and gave him harsh insults and well-placed whacks. When this happened, Juanito, a boy of eleven summers, became – at least in his mother's eyes – a newborn baby who wept helplessly. This turned his mother into a wounded she-wolf, and she attacked her husband fiercely. The little angel would smile to himself as his weeping grew louder and his skin took on a pomegranate tinge.

This morning, that's exactly what happened. The woman said, "Now take him to the zoo, Juan, for making him cry. Look at him, poor baby... don't you feel bad to see him like this? C'mon. Besides, when was the last time you took him somewhere?" With the shell of a macho man and the heart of a pigeon, Juan couldn't say no. He imagined his wife grabbing a frying pan, her body wrapped in a flower-print robe, her hair dyed and crowned with pastel blue curlers – how terrifying! So he only mumbled, "Yes, my love, of course. I'm taking him right now."

*   *   *

The sweet little boy ran through the crowd, his stiff hair a dark, flowerless cactus. He ignored his father when he shouted, "Wait, Juanito, not so fast. Don't get lost!" The boy didn't stop until he tripped over a gnawed corncob and fell flat on his face in a pink puddle. Puke or ice cream? The child stayed flat, uncertain whether to laugh, cry, or get up as if nothing had happened. He felt no pain, but he was so used to bursting into tears for any reason that it felt strange not to cry. Besides, his cotton candy was spoiled. With some difficulty he turned his head and looked for his papa in the forest of unfamiliar legs. Fifty yards or so away he saw him coming, his long thin legs supporting his bulky body, like a mosquito that had swallowed a chickpea. The same silhouette was already apparent in the boy's body – an irrefutable proof of paternity.

"C'mon, you little bastard. See what happens when you ignore me? Serves you right!"

This helped the child make up his mind – yes, he was going to cry. But unlike his saintly *mamacita*, his father didn't soften up to his crocodile tears. Did that vile man have no heart? Nonetheless, the boy persisted with his tearful appeal – however ineffectual, it still felt good. Don Juan stood beside the boy, who lay sobbing on the ground, completely unhurt. It was a Sunday, and the two wore tennis shoes and casual clothes. The father's eyes followed a miniskirt, but the sobbing from the fruit of his love became louder, weakening his stoic resolve to ignore the boy. His heart was not broken – his eardrums, yes. At that moment, the image of his wife with curlers and a frying pan came back to him. He decided to give in one last time.

"Juanelo, stop crying. You didn't get hurt, did you? Let's go, *mijo*. Up you go!"

In reply, his son gave a sharp cry, the enraged squawk of a capuchin monkey tantalized by a bunch of bananas. The father almost lost his patience; then he decided to offer a bribe – the plan B of every good father.

"If you get up, I'll buy you a double ice cream. Even better, why don't I take you to see the polar bear, Juanito? We're almost there, where the wild animals are, but you can't let the bear see you sniveling. So, why don't you hush now?"

The child stopped crying right away, and got up without difficulty. His eyes were drier than a camel's hooves. He put his fat little hands on his hips, the living image of the animated jug of Kool Aid. "I'd prefer a banana split. And where did you say I can see the little bear?"

*   *   *

"The gods must have created humans to torment the animals," the polar bear thought. He stretched out on the bluish white cement slab – a crudely painted imitation of an iceberg – and narrowed his eyes in the soft sun. Facedown, with his white rear standing up like a small snow-white volcano, he tried to rest. He wanted to spare his sensitive ears the clamor of the zoo visitors who clustered before his cage, unaware of his discomfort. But his efforts were in vain: the crowds of people were more annoying than a swarm of enraged bees, more difficult to endure than the pincers of an army of hungry crabs, more intolerable than an invasion of ticks in the most inaccessible and sensitive places of his white body, more... The polar bear's train of thought came to a halt when a small stone struck him in the face. Feeling drowsy in the midday sun, but clearly annoyed, he tried to pick out his tormentor's face among the monster of a thousand heads. Wasn't it enough that he put up with the heat, the awful food, the captivity? Must he also endure being stoned? In the great mass of bodies – skinny ones, fat ones, bodies clothed in T-shirts of every possible color – and faces – some with bronzed skin, some looking stupider than others – and in the midst of the racket and the terrible human stench (he had a highly attuned sense of smell), he found his enemy. It was a human cub, an ugly one indeed, with an extremely unpleasant odor, like a mixture of rotten fruit, rancid fish, and burned lard. The quarrelsome child laughingly celebrated the heroic feat of hitting the bear with the stone. The father of his attacker – the bear could make out a certain shared genetic ugliness – came close to the child and whispered in his ear, making him smile.

The polar bear, faking indifference, got up from his cement iceberg and took a drink of water. He moved slowly to the front of the cell and collapsed nonchalantly near the bars. In its splendor, his white fur resembled a cloud made of sugar cubes. His great claws were hidden beneath the silky white coat. The sight was truly delightful: the beast looked just like the star of a certain multinational soft drink company's Christmas advertising campaign. With unusual agility, Juanito climbed up on the small railing and planted his feet in the small space next to the sign that read *Danger – No Entry*. He leaned over the hedge that separated the crowd from the bars. A model citizen, Don Juan had wandered off to look for a trash bin in which to put the remains of the ice cream, while the zoo's security guards sipped soft drinks in plastic bags under the shade of a thick tree. No one paid any attention to the little boy who, with a eucalyptus branch, tried to poke the resident of the fenced cubicle.

Things happened so fast no one could do anything, but later everyone would recall the event as if it had happened in slow motion: the polar bear reached out a paw and snatched up his robust tormentor, pulling him roughly between the bars with his muzzle, until the boy was inside the cage. Of course, the unhappy cherub lost his life in the process: he was too large to cross the majestic threshold in one piece. But the white beast didn't eat him – his diet consisted strictly of fish, and the foul-smelling creature made him want to puke! He only played with the boy's lifeless body, tearing it slowly to pieces. The polar bear, now resembling a bloodstained peppermint, plunged slowly into the cold water and took a refreshing bath. The police arrived and someone called the ambulance. But it was too late: even the boy's clothing was unfit for recycling. Shutterbugs from the supermarket tabloids, however, would take delight in the sordid images.

After filling out the necessary paperwork, the exhausted Don Juan was finally allowed to go home. At the zoo entrance he ran into his wife, who was surrounded by reporters and TV cameras. She had arrived at the zoo in a frantic state, and had no idea what to say or do. Her makeup was ruined by tears, and she didn't know whether to embrace her husband, or punch him. She asked him how it had happened.

"I just told him it was the Coca-Cola polar bear, the one who gives away soft drinks in the Christmas parade. I think the kid was thirsty."

without ever pausing to offer thanks to the cook with the wide hips and tired eyes. In a few minutes, her routine will start, a job with no salary, no reward, and no gratitude; a labor nobody notices, except when she's sick and can't do it anymore.

That morning she woke up feeling certain she existed. She glanced at the clock and saw that she still had a couple of minutes before the annoying alarm filled the room with the sound of buzzing flies. She wrapped herself up in the sheets and considered her options. Committing suicide had always appealed to her, but she knew she couldn't go through with it: deep down she was a coward, fearful of pain. She was a Catholic, too, albeit a doubtful one, and she worried about the fate that awaited her on the other side. Killing her husband, however, was much more tempting. Once he was out of the picture, a great burden would be lifted from her. But there were also the children to think about: bumping off a husband is certainly judged severely, but murdering kids – no matter how unpleasant, lazy, and ungrateful they are – would be considered unforgivable. She couldn't do it. Going down in history as a black widow was one thing, but appearing on *Mexico's Most Wanted* as a bad mother, a Medea in an apron, was something she couldn't allow. Still, there were other options to consider…

The alarm clock, an infallible metal rooster, echoes through the bedroom. Next to her, her corpulent husband begins to stir. When he turns to tell her that he fancies his eggs with chorizo this morning, she can feel his foul morning breath on her face. She gets up, pulls on her daisy-print bathrobe, and heads down to the kitchen. She'll have time to think later.

On the upper edge of the window, the snail loses its grip and falls to the cobbled ground, landing with a thud. That day, the certainty that she existed fades slowly, like the hours of the morning.

The Scorpion of Almond

Laureano puts one bag of figs and another of quinces on the clay floor of the kitchen. He dabs at his sweaty forehead with a rag and leans against the wall of cantera stone to cool off. Outside, the humid sky turns gray and drops of rain start to fall, big and heavy like the early figs.

"The *patrona* says you must clean the hallway, cut the weeds in the garden, and then come and help me with the quince jelly. But first I want you to fetch me the copper saucepan from the attic," the cook says in a flat tone, as if the seasoning were missing from her voice.

Laureano nods and begins to walk slowly toward the attic staircase, stumbling over his seventy years and the gaps in the cobblestones. At the bottom of the pitted wooden stairs, the old man sighs as if preparing to encounter something significant. A few steps up, when it has become impossible to distinguish the creaking of the wood from that of his joints, Laureano feels an odd sensation on his hand, near the third knuckle. Looking down, he sees a slender scorpion with a reddish back. "It's one of the yellow ones," he murmurs to himself, trembling.

He had come to Durango at the age of five, when his father sought his fortune in the mining business. Once, on his birthday, he received a scorpion made of almond sugar paste. His mother had warned him that a real scorpion would kill him instantly. During all those years in Durango, and until this very day, Laureano has been lucky enough to dodge the deadly scorpions. Still, there are some dates that cannot be avoided.

The creature begins to crawl up the old man's arm. Just as the sting pierces his flesh, Laureano recalls the distant past and cries childishly.

That year, the quince jelly tastes bitter. A sign hangs in the kitchen window: *Full-time servant wanted, with references.*

Cookie Monster

The flock of girls sped away on roller skates. They were between eight and ten years old, their ponytails swaying in the breeze, their shoulders showing through their sleeveless blouses, their skin baked by the afternoon sun. I spent what seemed like an hour watching them. Fearful that someone might notice my delight, the stupid look on my face – so much beauty before my eyes! – I went to buy an ice cream. I nibbled at it, trying to dispel my thoughts and refresh my body. A day like any other.

It was always like that. Sitting on a park bench, I would pretend to be immersed in a book open at a random page, a book I never read. Around me, boys and girls played freely, as unsuspecting as pigeons strutting around the plaza. To the children, I was the man on the bench, nothing more than a familiar statue, a part of the landscape. No one paid any attention to me. Once, when a friendly boy sat down next to me and asked what I was reading, his smooth leg barely touching mine, no one noticed the way the blood surged through my veins, burning my cheeks red. My trembling hand brushed against his thigh as if by accident. I put my arm around his shoulders and briefly stroked his hair, telling him fairy tales to keep him beside me.

Let the children come to me. Who said that? I would wait for hours to see a small cherub bend over to tie his shoes, his butt sticking up, the shorts exposing his legs – a vision that gave me goose bumps. I would offer them help under the guise of paternal concern. I crouched down in front of them to tie their shoes. Sticky as a snail's trail, my glance slid along their small bodies. I knelt at their feet for as long as I could, my hands caressing those tiny ankles. I wished time would slow down so I could engrave the images of those angels on my mind. They said thank you, not suspecting they would later become the objects of my fantasies. Other times, I would bring a bag of cookies to tempt the children's appetites. They approached me, I gave them cookies, and my hand brushed against their naked arms, their necks. They flashed open smiles. A quiet, disturbing feeling would boil up inside me, intense, hard to control. I feared I would slobber like a lunatic and run after the children, my arms outstretched like a cartoon monster, ridiculous yet dangerous.

But I always managed to control myself. I kept the feelings and images inside until I came home, until my wife went out shopping. Only then, with the bathroom door locked in case my wife returned early, could I release my desires. I had never dared go beyond my fantasies. I didn't think there was anything wrong with the way I felt, with my preferences, but I knew no one would understand me. They would condemn me, and wish me a slow, painful death. So I always stayed celibate in that sense: sex inside marriage didn't count because it meant nothing to me; it was an obligation like any other. Yes, I could always keep my true yearnings at bay and channel them when I was alone. That had always been my intention. I never wanted to harm anyone. That is, until the first time. After that, I couldn't control my impulses.

That afternoon, my life changed. I guess some would say it was the moment I turned into what I am now: a monster. The disturbing feeling aroused by the flock of roller skaters couldn't be dispelled by the ice cream, or a long walk, or a cold shower, or a televised soccer game. It was as if someone had made a decision for me. And now everything that happened seemed like a dream, a dream where I had no control over anything and was at the mercy of some unknown force.

A package of cookies and the promise of a toy were all I needed to persuade the hungry-eyed boy to accompany me to the lonely spot. He might have been seven or eight, it was hard to tell. His body was small, thin, malnourished, but there was something about his eyes that made him look much older. Maybe that's why he wasn't surprised when I touched him. He seemed to understand that everything had its price, and he paid that price with admirable stoicism. I'd like to believe I didn't hurt him much. I kissed him gently and began to run my hands all over his body. A sweet sensation gradually filled me, and feelings I had never experienced before surged through me. I touched him, fondled him, and made him do the same to me. He responded clumsily, but managed to bring me to ecstasy. Then everything ended, and the world turned gray. Suddenly I wanted to be alone. I left the boy in front of the shopping center, pressing a banknote into his hand so he could buy himself a toy.

When I went home that night, I feared my wife would take one look at my face and know what had happened – but it didn't turn out that way. Our lives carried on as usual, but I was never the same again. I had corrupted a child with my money and my caresses. I had become Cookie Monster.

A Perfect Day for Canned Tuna

Susana is a housewife, but she could have been a porn actress or an executive secretary. It's not as if her life led her to a fork in the road and she took the path marked *Domestic Goddess*: it's more like she was pushed off the roof of a building. She grew up uneventfully in a middle-class family, but after her father ran away one fine day – he didn't even bother to stick to the cliché and tell everyone he was going out for cigarettes – she had to contribute to the household. Back then she was still in high school and dreamed of a life beyond domesticity. But because she was the oldest sister, her plans for college turned into a diploma course at a night school for secretaries, and a crazy teenage life – she felt entitled to some fun – which included a series of low-paying jobs at fast-food joints and behind the counters of small shops.

There are days when her past life seems so far away, and then there are others, like today, when she feels like it was just last week. "I could touch it if I tried," she thinks, as she hears Enrique come home and sit down at the kitchen table. He doesn't greet her with a kiss like those couples in the TV commercials, but that's fine with her: she hasn't had a shower and doesn't want anyone to come near her when she's all sweaty. Susana places a bowl of vegetable soup in front of him. A look of frustration crosses his face, but he grabs the spoon and begins to eat. She knows she's not exactly the best cook in the world, not even a second-rate one, but he's not the type who throws the plate at the wall when he finds his food bland.

Susana watches him swallow the mass of overcooked vegetables and chicken. She takes a seat in front of him and asks how his day went. Enrique, who works for the Treasury Department and has no problem sharing his life, launches into a detailed account of the audit of a strip joint. Susana, who only asked out of politeness, begins to wash a pot stained yellow with grease. She too took her clothes off for money. She never told him, but when she was seventeen a friend from work invited her to make a comic book: he would be in charge of the text and she of the images. Susana told him she wasn't good at drawing, but her friend told her it didn't matter because they would be using photos. When she learned that she would be paid as much as she normally earned in two months of taking orders for burgers and fries, her doubts melted away. They met in an apartment in a trendy neighborhood, where a photographer took photos of her sucking her friend's cock – due to budget constraints, her friend doubled as writer and leading man. His ass was covered with acne and he wasn't in the habit of taking a daily shower. Susana had to touch herself, show her tits to the camera, and lick her lips. The photographer paid her in cash and told her the magazine would be sold only in Mexico City, but three months later, when Susana was walking downtown with her mother and fifteen-year-old brother, she saw a photo of herself at the newsstand, wearing excessive makeup and gaping like a Munch figure. The paper was porous and she looked haggard. A speech bubble above her head read: "Fuck me hard, *papi.*"

"What's next?" asks Enrique, pushing his empty dish aside.

"I made a soufflé, but I burned it."

Her husband sighs. They have never talked about separation. Even during their worst quarrels, she's never told him to leave and he's never threatened to do that. She feels happy to be with him, but how can this be true? He doesn't even get angry: if he did, they could fight and perhaps get a divorce. But she has a real problem coping with other people's anger. It's not something she's proud of, but she knows it defines who she is, like her slightly crooked teeth and shrill voice. When someone gets mad at her, she will do anything to placate that person. But Enrique almost never loses his temper. Now he wants to see the soufflé, saying, "Maybe it's not so bad." Susana bends over to open the oven door. With her apron tied around her waist she looks like one of those happy housewives from the '50s, promoting the latest line of electrical appliances. The oven reveals a dark mass of charred vegetables.

Susana puts her hands on the table. The polish on her nails is chipped. She hasn't had a chance to shave her legs. Her husband examines what's left of his main dish. She knows she doesn't look like the woman Enrique married almost a decade ago, when a fey young man did her hair and makeup, and her dress was right out of a bridal magazine. She was the envy of her girlfriends, who dreaded becoming old maids: their jealousy pinched her, like her shoes with their pointed tips. What else has happened to them, besides so many breakfasts with coffee, the daily routine of couples living under the same roof? What else, besides the death of countless cells over the years? Susana had been Enrique's secretary for a while. He fell in love with her, and instead of taking advantage of her, he asked for her hand and took her out of work – the dream of all her female coworkers, who were stuck in the office preparing bitter coffee and exploiting the company's Xerox machine for personal use.

They never talk about separation, but it hangs over their heads all the time, like a guillotine. For Susana, it's the secret weapon, the final solution. But the blade isn't large or sharp, nor does it hang by a thin thread. It wouldn't cut off anyone's head. If it fell, it would sound like a pin dropping on the floor. Maybe some angels would fly away, but nothing more. Enrique stands up and rummages through the pantry like a bee inside a flower. When he comes out, he has a can of tuna in his hand. He puts it on the table and looks for the mayonnaise and bread.

"I think today is a perfect day for canned tuna," he says, a can opener in his hand. Susana has to agree with her husband.

Bacon and Eggs

The background music murmurs like the sea on a distant shore. No one listens to it, but it muffles all other sounds. Like ants who can't find their way back to the nest, people weave around the room, chatting, roaring with laughter, cups and glasses in their hands. As they down their drinks, women lose their composure and begin flirting with other women's husbands. Men gather in groups, smoking cigars and telling raunchy jokes, bragging about their latest conquests. A small crowd clusters around a gypsy woman hired by the hosts to read cards for the guests. As night deepens, the women's makeup begins to run, and their salon-styled hairdos start to resemble lions' manes. Tobacco smoke fills the air, mingling with the scent of so many different perfumes – and with the unmistakable smell of *woman*, which disgusts you.

You stand close to the appetizers, chugging down one beer after another. You flash the hostess a satisfied smile and she looks at you, mouthing, "How are you?" You pretend to listen to a group of men, but as soon as you see that the gypsy woman is alone, you hurry toward her. Surprised, she raises her head. As she gathers the cards from the table, she looks you up and down. Suddenly, you're aware of your alcohol-puffed face, your short stature, your two hundred and sixty pounds. Your fat fingers begin tapping on your brown corduroy pants, and your double chin rests on your shirt collar, waiting. Finally, the woman gives you a nervous smile and gestures for you to sit down in front of her. With hands as brown and spotted as cinnamon cookies, she shuffles the cards and turns them over one by one – all Jacks.

"Do you have boyfriends, male lovers?" Her voice is clear and high, but her tone is doubtful.

"No, of course not. Well, sometimes I fantasize about it, but no, I haven't really done it."

The gypsy woman flips over a few more cards and freezes, staring at the upside down Ace of Spades. Her eyes remain unblinking for a few seconds, and then her lips move without any sound: "Danger." You read her lips and ask what's wrong. You feel uncomfortable, but intrigued.

"It's nothing. I think I made a mistake. I'll shuffle the cards again."

She repeats the routine. This time she turns over the Ace of Diamonds.

"Have you had any trouble with the law lately?"

"Just a ticket for failing to stop at a stop sign. How did you know?" You smile, your small blue eyes disappearing into your fat cheeks. The woman breathes harder, her face turning red, and you notice her hands are trembling as she hurries to gather up the cards. She brings her hand to her throat and stares at you like a frightened animal. She doesn't say anything more about your cards. Claiming to have another engagement, she leaves the room. Outside, she throws her cards in the bushes and runs as fast as her skinny legs can carry her.

*   *   *

The children's legs were also skinny, as reed-like as the legs of herons and flamingos. But this did not lend them the appearance of grace: instead, only poignancy emanated from those frail, hairless creatures with their deep, dark eyes. Clad, as always, in your bright-colored costume – one red trouser leg, one blue, with a yellow torso – and with your face painted like a clown's, you entertained kids with terminal diseases. Dressed in their pale blue hospital gowns, they laughed with you. And for a moment they seemed to forget about their cancer, about the IV fluids dripping into their veins, about their yellowish-gray skin, the unbearable pains, the sedatives, the faces offering gifts and flowers, and about the mothers who smothered their cries and forced their trembling lips to smile. And, immersed in your role as model citizen, you also forgot your problems – the worries that had been gnawing at your guts for as long as you could remember, and the strain of pretending to your wife, always pretending.

"Everything all right, darling?" The hostess, a good friend of you and your wife, offers whiskey on the rocks, flashing her perfect white teeth. You take the glass and return her smile. How long have you been standing there with an empty beer can in your hand?

"And the gypsy woman?"

"She said she had to go. She had another engagement," you answer, and empty your glass in one gulp.

"Oh, what a shame! I wanted her to read my cards, too. You know, I think Esteban is cheating on me. Oh, honey, you don't know how I feel. You don't know anything, do you? No, of course not. You'd have told me."

"No, I know nothing about it. But if I were you, I wouldn't

believe what a gypsy woman says. It's fun, but you shouldn't take it seriously. She told me a bunch of nonsense, things that aren't true."

"Really? I'm so desperate to believe in anything, honey. But thank you for telling me. I'll just have to use other methods to find out if Esteban is seeing someone."

"Have you seen Rosalinda? I'm not feeling well. You know, my ulcer is acting up again, but I don't want to spoil the party for her. She's having a good time. Please tell her I've gone home. I'm sure she won't mind."

"Of course I'll tell her. And Rosalinda can spend the night here, so no one has to drive drunk. Besides, you know your wife and I are best friends. It's no problem."

*   *   *

"No problem," your mother said, when you found your dog chewing your father's velvet slippers. She picked up the pieces scattered on the floor and prayed that her husband wouldn't miss them that night: the next day she would go out and buy the same slippers. You were only seven, and the incident didn't worry you. You were having a glass of milk and a peanut butter sandwich for dinner when you heard a scream. Your mother rubbed her hands on her imaginary apron, and a familiar shadow of fear crossed her face. Then you found out that the miserable dog had puked right in front of your father's reclining chair, a mixture of gastric juice, croquettes, and bits of slipper. Your father seized you by the neck with one hand and grabbed the dog with the other. He dragged you both outside to the backyard. Then he pulled out a gun and shot the dog four times before your eyes – the first shot went through the ribs and made it whimper like a puppy; another shot to the head splashed its brain over the green grass; two more shots to the body finished it off. You began to whimper, fearing that your father would shoot you next. But he didn't do it. Instead, he slapped you, and your tears flew through the dark night air like glowworms. Your cheeks burned as he warned you, "I'm only doing this to teach you a lesson. Don't touch my things. And don't cry like a girl. Stop crying, you fucking faggot! You're going to be a fag when you grow up if you cry like that, goddamn it. It was just a dog."

*   *   *

It's just a dog, but you brake suddenly in front of the starving mongrel. It wobbles across the street, its hide ridden with mange, its rib cage like accordion pleats, death stalking its bald tail. You take a deep breath and start the van again, driving slowly, as if navigating a small boat through winding canals. At dawn, the city looks different, humid and dimly lit, and this makes you feel relaxed. You light a cigarette and notice a young boy under a streetlamp. Moths flutter about and smash against the light, sprinkling golden dust on the boy's tilted head. He looks no older than sixteen. He senses your interest and wiggles his hips sheathed in black leather shorts. You stop and open the van's passenger door for him. The boy sits next to you and mumbles an amount that seems reasonable.

During the ride home, your companion remains silent. You smoke, sneaking glimpses at the boy out of the corner of your eye. Dark skin, gray-green eyes, brown hair, a long, perfect body. He reeks of pot and cheap cologne, but you don't mind much. Satisfied with your choice, you let out a discreet burp and ask his name, knowing that what he tells you will be a lie. You fix your eyes on the road, making small talk about the weather, the recent heat wave. As you drive along the central reservation, ragged rows of *sahuayos* flash by the car window.

*   *   *

"Are they prickly pears, too?" you asked, excited, as the gray car sped along the rural road, heading for the vast, empty desert. Javier, a family friend, smiled and stroked your head, messing up your hair. "No, they're a type of cactus. They're called *sahuayos*. Look how big they are!" he said, running a hand up and down your thighs. Suddenly, the car stopped in a small clearing. You looked around and saw only the sand and the army of *sahuayos*, silent witnesses who looked on, indifferent, as your father's friend began to tickle you. You twisted your body, a pained look on your face. His tickles became caresses, and his fingers slithered into your Bermuda shorts like an army of slugs. You cried, "No, no, please don't!" His fingers crawled over your testicles. Despite your fear, your small penis grew hard inside his hand, and, encouraged by this, he unzipped his fly. You gagged as his penis touched the back of your throat. As he held your head down, you thought about the *sahuayos*, and about the desert animals you'd seen in picture books.

* * *

The van screeches to a halt in front of your house. The boy, distracted, is thrown against the dashboard. You apologize and tell him shyly that you have arrived.

Inside, you fix a couple of drinks, put on a porn flick, and invite the boy to lie down next to you on the bed. Both of you end up naked after a few sips of alcohol. You act out all your fantasies. In the end, you offer to pay him more to spend the night with you; after all, Rosalinda won't be home until noon tomorrow. After panting, sweat, and satisfaction, you both fall into a deep sleep.

* * *

At first, you thought the man was asleep. When you started working for the funeral parlor, you had a hard time being around the dead bodies. They seemed almost alive, and so vulnerable. You were afraid of undressing them, cleaning them, laying them out in the clothes their families had chosen, and putting makeup on them, but the dead submitted to you without resistance. One day your boss went out, leaving you alone. Without knowing how, you found yourself caressing the young man's cold, naked body. You pretended he was just asleep and had somehow invited your sexual advances. You came inside the dead body many times, ripping his tight muscles. In the end, exhausted from your efforts, you fell asleep on top of him, and there was no time to pull a sheet across your naked body when your boss came into the room. That was your last day at work.

* * *

A small noise wakes you. It takes you a few seconds to remember what happened last night. You grope across the bed, but find it empty. Still naked, you rise to look for the boy, fearing that he has made off with some electronic appliance or your wallet. You hurry to the kitchen and find him there. He is holding a knife in his hand and steps toward you, smiling. You react immediately, snatching the knife away before he can do anything. You notice you have accidentally cut his arm, and dark, thick blood drips from the wound. He looks at you with frightened eyes as you lift the knife to your lips and, without thinking, lick the bloody blade. The boy tries to push past you, striking your face with his wounded arm. Then you see your own hand plunge the knife into his hairless chest. You realize you can't stop; you have to repeat the action over and over until you exhaust your strength. You drop the knife, his body, and your eyes. Your chest heaving, you notice you've had the biggest orgasm of your life. Just at that moment, your eyes settle on the blood-splattered kitchen counter. There, spread out on the cutting board, you notice a few slices of cold bacon and a carton of eggs.

"It's too late now," you mumble, as you bend over to clean the floor, trying not to think of what you'll repeat again and again.

The Avon Lady

He's never seen a naked dwarf, but he's thought about it a few times since he met her. His stomach feels like an aquarium swarming with restless fish. Who can blame him – it's many men's fantasy.

Mariquita pours coffee into blue-striped ceramic cups – her best cups. She sets out the cream container, spoons, and sugar cubes. Then she gets down from the stool and walks across the room, balancing the tray without spilling a drop. She sets it down on the coffee table, and Rodrigo smiles at her as he takes one of the cups. His forearms and the backs of his hands are like a black rug. She looks down at the floor. Laura had referred to this as "my husband's hair problem."

Mariquita prepares her coffee, and looks up at Rodrigo through the rising steam. "Your wife?"

She doesn't usually ask the men about their wives or girlfriends – it would be impolite – but today is different. It can't be a coincidence that Rodrigo has turned up at her house that morning, freshly bathed and smelling of expensive aftershave.

"She's home. I was leaving for work, but I saw that you forgot this and I thought I'd drop it off on my way to the office." Rodrigo points to the cardboard Avon box at his feet. He picks it up and places it at Mariquita's feet, which dangle from the chair, far above the floor. The box is full of cosmetics and perfumes: she had left it on purpose a few days ago.

"And how is she?"

"You know, elegant and tyrannical as always." Rodrigo is the type of man who fails miserably when he tries to be ironic.

Mariquita laughs discreetly and sips her coffee as she studies Rodrigo. He's a good-looking, burly man with black eyebrows like leather stoles. She feels herself getting wet, and crosses and uncrosses her legs to ease the sensation. She's as horny as a robust regular-sized woman. As she shifts in her seat, she drops her spoon on the floor. She leans over to pick it up. Her low-cut blouse reveals the backward parentheses of her breasts – perfect-B boobs, which are equivalent to a double D-cup on her body. Rodrigo ogles her, of course. Mariquita hasn't met anyone who doesn't do that. Rodrigo is faster and hands her the spoon. She sits up, smiling at him.

"It's very nice of you to bring my things."

"Well, I imagine if they were left at my house, I'd have to pay for them."

Ah, he plays a man in charge of his finances. He's afraid of getting to the point. Why doesn't he tell her he wanted to see her?

"Well, you're very kind. I have several clients' orders in there."

Rodrigo wipes his face with his hand, as if cleaning gummy eyes. Only then does he stop staring at her breasts and smile at her.

He clears his throat and scratches the back of his neck. It seems as if all men were programmed to do this. Sometimes seduction can be as tedious as the sales pitch she has to recite to persuade her clients to buy the anti-wrinkle cream.

"You're a very attractive woman, despite…" He regrets his choice of words before he even finishes. "I mean, when I saw you in my house, you seemed very…"

She moves closer and stops in front of Rodrigo's legs.

"There are more than eighty types of dwarves. I'm one of the few who are proportionate. My face is normal."

"Your face is beautiful."

"And you're very attractive." Mariquita, only a few inches away, takes a breath. "Men like you always smell nice."

Rodrigo seems to relax a little. When someone is as good-looking as that, he can't help attracting women's attention. He takes Mariquita and sits her on his lap. He kisses her like a mother bird feeding a worm to her young.

*   *   *

Laura had spent the morning watching a Mexican movie and two infomercials. One hawked a wonderful soap for weight loss; the other, a vegetable cutter that was said to be the answer to all nutrition problems. She was jotting down the toll-free number to order the products when she heard the doorbell ring. Then she realized her feet were numb and she was still in her nightdress. She took it off, shouted, "Just a moment," and put on yesterday's clothes as fast as she could.

She opened the door. At first she didn't see anyone and thought some of the neighborhood kids were playing ding-dong ditch on her again. But immediately she noticed a silhouette by the flowerpot of geraniums. She saw a tiny woman carrying a huge Avon box.

"Ding dong, Avon calling."

Laura had to let her in. Not only was the woman small, but she was also gorgeous, and seemed to have a sense of humor. Besides, Laura had been feeling lonely lately. She could use someone to talk to. For months, she and Rodrigo had exchanged only a few words: *Have you seen my shirt? I'm sure it's still where you left it. I only wash what's in the basket. You didn't buy green tea? I don't drink that kind of tea, so I didn't realize we were out. Did you put it on the shopping list?* She read in *Vanidades* that this type of communication was a form of passive aggression.

Laura led the tiny woman into the kitchen, which was usually the cleanest place in her house. Rodrigo had done all the dishes, cleaned the table, and taken the garbage out before he went to work. Whenever he was fed up, he would do household chores. A real angel, as her mother-in-law would say.

Gesturing for the saleswoman to sit, Laura took her own seat, ready to buy whatever was offered. Why shouldn't she buy something if it would make her feel better? Besides, any excuse would do to look at this wonder of nature — because the dwarf woman *was* a wonder. And she was also very young. She had wonderful skin. Suddenly, Laura felt embarrassed about her own looks. She had messy hair, no makeup, wrinkled clothes, unpainted toes, and morning breath. Everything around her seemed dreadful, out of place, even her five-foot-five-inch stature, which had once been her pride. The tiny saleswoman, on the other hand, was the embodiment of perfection. Laura felt like crying.

The little woman finished arranging all her products on the table and looked at the housewife in front of her. Underneath the extra forty pounds she carried, she still had a certain beauty, altered by her domesticity. The Avon lady noticed that the house was in a deplorable condition, much like its owner. Cobwebs clouded the corners of the walls. A thick layer of dust covered every visible surface. There was even roach shit in some corners. You could see the layers of this woman's depression in the months of accumulated clutter.

"My name is María, but everyone calls me Mariquita. I don't know why."

Laura bent forward to listen. A few seconds later, she laughed. She hadn't laughed about something so simple before, and instantly felt foolish. She held out her hand to the Avon lady.

"I'm Laura."

Mariquita didn't shake her hostess's hand. She just left her hand in Laura's palm for a few seconds, like a dead fish, then withdrew it before she finished her greeting.

"I think I've got just what you need."

"Something to cheer me up? Tips to spice up my marriage? The meaning of life? I'm so bitter," Laura thought. She could barely manage a smile. She was on the verge of tears.

"What's the matter?" asked the tiny woman. "Nine out of ten women feel better about themselves when they're smartly dressed. Did you know that?"

Laura answered with a fake smile. Mariquita had offended her and piqued her interest at the same time. At this point in her life, any solution was welcome.

"May I offer you a makeup session? It's free, there's no obligation. If you don't feel better, I'll give you the product of your choice."

"Maybe she didn't mean to offend me," Laura thought. The tiny saleswoman is just trying to earn her bread. It's true, Laura isn't exactly a supermodel. Or rather, as Rodrigo said the last time they quarreled, she looks like an old hag.

"Let's have a cup of coffee first," she said.

"Okay. I'm in no hurry."

"Real sugar or artificial sweeteners?" Laura asked, as she began to wash the coffee pot.

"Sugar is fine." Mariquita spread out a napkin on the table. She noticed suspicious stains on the tablecloth. "What's troubling you, dear?"

*　　*　　*

They eagerly shed their clothes. Rodrigo doesn't have a married man's body. He's in good shape, and this makes Mariquita think she isn't the first woman with whom he has cheated on his wife. The first dwarf, of course, but not the first woman. Even though she uses a diaphragm, she's going to need extra protection. Handsome men are the raw material of venereal diseases.

Laura's husband presses his face into Mariquita's crotch. Like all the men she has tried before, he whips his tongue around, as if "fast and furious" were synonymous with orgasm. She knows to put up with it for a while and then feign a quick orgasm so he'll stop. The least he could do is to shave. A true gentleman is considerate. Rodrigo seems excited, lifting Mariquita up in the air while he goes down on her. Men are very simple creatures.

Mariquita makes a time-out sign with her hands. He gently places her on the sofa. She looks inside her purse.

"What's wrong?"

"Lie down there." She points to the carpet. Rodrigo obeys, thinking of Laura. He remembers when they used to make love, when she knew what he wanted, what he needed. Back then, Laura was still thin and ambitious. She had a sparkle in her eyes.

Mariquita has seen much larger penises, but this one isn't too bad. It's average. Besides, the men with the super-sized cocks always worry about hurting her. There's nothing better than showing them that her vagina is much deeper than a normal-sized woman's – it always surprises them. They stare at her with a confused look. She puts a condom on Rodrigo, and he murmurs, "Oh, not that." He's just a little boy at heart, like all men.

"Yes, because you never know." Some men pretend to take offence, but Rodrigo is the type who gives in too soon. He's so desperate to fuck her that he's willing to make some concession.

Rodrigo has moles on his neck, making him look like a chocolate chip cookie. He enjoys watching Mariquita's breasts bounce up and down while she straddles him.

*   *   *

"Would you like a cookie?"

"Yes, please."

Between cups of coffee and too many carbohydrates, the two women chatted like life-long friends. Then Mariquita returned to her role as Avon lady, putting makeup on Laura and fixing her hair. When she handed her a mirror, Laura couldn't recognize herself: it wasn't her. Her shiny red lips trembled. She hadn't felt so good for a long time. That's why she browsed through the catalogs and bought practically everything Mariquita suggested.

That day, they had talked only about Laura's marriage. Better than therapy, it had been cathartic for her. She felt strong, assertive, and full of plans. She had a clear future goal. She decided to start a new diet and put on makeup every day. Everything was going to change. First *she* would change, and then her relationship with Rodrigo and everything else.

"Will you be back soon, Mariquita?" Laura wanted to order other products and talk to her more. She had so many questions she wanted to ask Mariquita.

Rodrigo came into the house and stopped on the threshold of the kitchen. He was hungry. The traffic was impossible. To find his wife looking like Penélope Cruz and chatting with a small woman was the last thing he expected. Rodrigo approached Laura, and she got up like a rusty hinge. He gave her a chaste peck on the forehead. The awkwardness of the scene resembled a photograph with the caption "Portrait of a husband and wife: ten years later."

When she had finished packing up her things, Mariquita walked up to Rodrigo and extended her hand from below. "You must be Rodrigo. I'm Mariquita."

Rodrigo stammered a response as Mariquita kissed Laura goodbye and promised to come back soon.

After the tiny woman was gone, Rodrigo was still speechless. That day he didn't care whether Laura had dinner ready or not. When he remembered he was hungry, he suggested they order pizza. That evening they made love for the first time in eight months.

* * *

"Like doing it with a doll." Rodrigo looks up at the ceiling of Mariquita's house. It's newly painted, and there are no cobwebs in the corners. Mariquita rests her head on Rodrigo's chest, her fingers playing in his hair. He turns his head. Recently watered flowerpots are scattered around the room. He thinks about his own home, where the few plants look like they're made of plastic. Here the walls are covered with Goya's lithographs and pictures in old frames. The people in the photos look like her, but none of them is a dwarf. The cuckoo clock on the wall tells him it's almost noon. It's time for him to leave.

"Well, I think…" He sits up in bed and looks around for his shirt.

"Thank you for bringing me my stuff." Mariquita kisses him on the neck. Outside it has started to rain – one of those autumn storms that come and go without warning. Rodrigo wishes he could stay there and sleep. Mariquita stands on the bed and gestures for him to come closer. Rodrigo obeys meekly. He would do anything she asks of him. Mariquita adjusts his tie with motherly affection. "Take care."

Rodrigo leaves the house and walks out the front door and across the garden. The rain bounces off the sidewalk. When he'd arrived, he hadn't noticed the small, bearded garden gnome standing by the flower hedge, a cap on its head. Soon the grass will be covered with mushrooms. The air smells of wet earth. Of Mariquita's sex. He wishes he had brought an umbrella.

Fish without a Bicycle

"Do you remember the rotten milk?" I ask my brother, who nods while keeping his eyes on the road. We're in my car on the way to visit our mother in the hospital, but he's behind the wheel, out of habit, I suppose. He always had to look after me, his baby sister. My brother would carry my backpack, help me with my math homework, and bring me a glass of water at any hour of the night. After all, Papa forced him to.

"She thought it was yogurt," he says, sipping on his bottle of water. He's always avoided coffee, alcohol, and drugs, and my fondness for such vices is one of the many reasons he disapproves of me.

"Nobody believes spoiled milk becomes yogurt."

"Raw, uncultured milk turns sour. I think Mama was just confused."

Communication has never been my brother Roberto's strong suit. He never calls and rarely answers e-mails. In person he offers technical jargon or monosyllabic answers, mere snippets of words, as if talking pains him – unless he needs to defend Mama, of course. Never mind that she made him drink rancid milk at breakfast for years.

"Don't you remember how she hit you when you spat it out in the sink?"

"It was the '80s. We couldn't afford to dump a gallon of milk down the drain."

"What are you saying? She didn't do us any harm?"

"She never meant to. That was never her intention."

I turn on the radio and tune it to a station offering soap updates and celebrity gossip. Now we stare ahead, both of us wearing the same stubborn look from years ago. I could keep shoving anecdotes up his nose, but he's always going to come up with some excuse for Mama. Papa, almost always away, didn't know about those struggles over the milk. When I told him about it, Mama stopped forcing me to drink it, but Roberto continued to be her victim – I don't know why.

My brother changes stations, finds a song, and taps his fingers against the steering wheel, lip-synching. I gobble down a chocolate doughnut I brought with me in a brown paper bag. I have to bribe myself with treats when I go to visit Mama, just like she used to bribe me when she took us to get vaccinated. I would howl all the way to the clinic until she offered to buy me a candy bar. My brother, on the other hand, received nothing except an explanation of the benefits of vaccination: "It's for your own good." He would hold out his arm without crying and, even though my mouth was smeared with chocolate, I felt like I was being deprived of something.

I noisily sip my overpriced coffee, knowing Roberto hates this sound. He keeps tapping the rhythm on the wheel, as if it's nothing, but when we pull into the hospital parking lot he brakes hard, and I fly off the seat, spilling my double mocha on my blouse.

*   *   *

The room reeks of cleaning fluid, but there's something even stronger – Mama's smell. It's a mixture of withered flowers, Channel, and the urine-like stench of penicillin – unless it's something worse. Roberto doesn't seem to notice it and launches himself toward the bed to kiss her. Her skin is sagging and almost transparent. I stand near the bed and ask her how she feels, but she puts out her arms and I have to bend down to let her hug me, putting up with her breath that smells like sauerkraut.

"Sweetheart, you look pretty in that," she says. I look at my coffee-stained blouse, pulled tight across my breasts. Sometimes I can't find bras in my size in Mexico and have to wait until Roberto crosses the border. Over there they make underwear for cows like me. Papa taught him never to refuse me a favor, and so he always brings me some. I imagine him wandering through the aisles filled with women, hesitating as he checks sizes, textures, and colors. A saleswoman asks him if he's looking for something for his wife or girlfriend, and he has to confess that he wants beige satin 38DD bras for his sister.

"It's dirty and too tight – you don't have to tell me."

My mother doesn't hear me because she's telling Roberto all the details of her convalescence. She was hospitalized a couple of weeks ago for abdominal pains that turned out to be tumors in her ovaries. The surgery left her weak, and now the doctors are keeping her under observation. Having recently lost weight, she's thinner than ever – but she still feels well enough to make me feel bad about myself. If I bring this up, Roberto will say, "Mama was just paying you a compliment. Why do you always get so defensive?"

A nurse comes in to take her vital signs and give her some pills. My mother lets the nurse work, giving her the faint, sweet smile she reserves for strangers; the one she never gave me. I sink into the visitor's chair and into the bitter darkness engulfing me. My brother comes over and whispers that Mama needs privacy – the nurse is going to change the sheets and give her a sponge bath.

*   *   *

In the hospital cafeteria, Roberto buys a juice for himself and a large black coffee for me. Then he joins me outside as I light a cigarette. My brother sits down beside me on the bench, even though the smoke irritates his throat.

"Do you remember when we were home alone and we jumped on to the beds from the top of the closet?"

"Of course I remember," he says, trying to wave the smoke away.

"And when we went out through the balcony and climbed over the fence in the backyard?"

He gives me a look that says 'I know where you're going with this' and nods. "I also remember we played outside with the other kids until it got dark. Things were different then, Elsa," he says.

True. Childhood obesity was almost unheard of when we were growing up. If I were a young girl today, I would pass for just another plump child in danger of diabetes, and nobody in the street would turn to look at me. But back then I was called *fatso* in school. I developed breasts in fourth grade and got my period in fifth. I was the butt of jokes among the other kids, and the street laborers hurled crude comments at me. My mother told me to pay no heed to those who teased me. "Don't stoop to their level, Elsa. A dignified person must ignore them." But I never felt dignified. I was ashamed of my body. I tried to hide my breasts and walk with a stoop, but it didn't help. Still, although having overdeveloped breasts was humiliating, I later learned that the flat-chested girls suffered even more.

"We were lucky nothing happened to us," I say.

*   *   *

When we go back to my mother's room, she's asleep. She breathes noisily, her mouth half open. A faint smell of vinegar floats in the air. The doctor opens the door and beckons us to come outside. He tells us that our mother has cancer. Although the tumors have been removed, it has spread to other parts of the body. Roberto asks about treatments, pain relief, and other options.

"How long does she have left?" I interrupt.

The doctor and Roberto give me a look that turns from surprise to scorn in a few seconds. It's a question that would be on anyone's mind, but it seems that putting it into words is like pushing a naked person onto the stage. It's very easy for my brother and the man in the white coat, with their education, their marriages and children, their functional households – households with a woman in charge – to judge me. In their masculine world, the old maid should be the one worrying about her dying mother. To them, I'm just my mother's daughter, nothing more. They've never visited the basement where I keep the emotional baggage my mother gave me, all of it covered in mold, dust, and resentment.

The night Papa died of a heart attack in the kitchen, I was in my room watching my favorite detective show and eating ice cream, my mother was arguing over a game of canasta at the house of one of her friends, and my brother was studying abroad. His death didn't seem to cause any distress, and I thought it would be the same with her.

"It depends on how she responds to the treatment," says the doctor. Before he leaves, he takes a quick glance at my blouse. My nipples have hardened under my clothes, betraying me in the cold air of the hospital corridor.

We go back to the room and I collapse into the chair, which swallows me and those mountains of shame. Roberto sits by Mama's bed and watches her sleep. He passes his hand through her hair and his fingers leave wide furrows of baldness. For the first time I wish I had a husband by my side, a couple of kids to look after, an excuse to divide our approaching suffering equally among us. My weight and my spinsterhood have always been the causes of the worst quarrels between my mother and me. "You need a man to take care of you" was her old mantra. She insisted that my brother – and my father, when he was alive – couldn't be by my side forever, and that I was useless by myself, a spoiled cow. When I went through my feminist phase, as all women do, I told her that a woman without a man is like a fish without a bicycle. I remember reading the line in some magazine. She stared up at me from her five-foot-five and one-hundred-twenty-pound frame, her makeup impeccable, and asked, "But what would the fish do when the bicycle needs repair? It would need a man."

Roberto says he can visit Mama every day after work, and ask for time off to take her to chemotherapy, but that she should stay with me. After all, that's her house – where would she feel more comfortable?

My silence is an unspoken acceptance. It's just like when we used to fight and she would tell us to apologize to each other: my brother was capable of saying sorry, but I would stare down at my feet without a word. Then he would come to me and say softly, "You'll forgive me, won't you, Elsa?" I would barely move my head, clenching my fists while my tears fell to the floor.

On the return trip, I crack open the window to let out the cigarette smoke. Roberto turns and says, "I'd never give my kids sour milk."

I smile in spite of myself.

The Canary

The restroom floor was covered with puke, and the front wall had been dotted with orange stains. The stink of liquor and frustration filled the air. Doña Mica knew where the stench came from, but she had put off cleaning up the mess until someone complained. She'd been cleaning restrooms for ten years, but she still hadn't managed to dull her sensitive nose, which was her weak spot, according to her supervisor. "Ah Mica, why did you choose this job if you're so delicate?" he would ask when he saw her trying to suppress the urge to vomit, hunched over like a cat coughing up a stubborn hairball. She would have to compose herself, take a deep breath, and say she was fine, that it was all right now and she would finish cleaning right away.

Doña Mica puts the container of bleach away and rinses the rags. As she removes her rubber gloves, one finger at a time, like milking a cow, she prays that the recently mopped floor will dry before someone comes and makes a mess of it again. There must be a saint she could ask for help in these worldly matters – who could it be? But it doesn't take long before some woman comes, squats over the toilet without letting her ass touching the seat, and sprays piss all over the place. Then the next woman has no choice but to piss spread-eagle. And so Mica has to clean the toilet for the fifteenth time today. The pain shoots through her back every evening when she finishes her shift. She picks up the loose change from the ashtrays in front of the mirrors. There are fewer coins now than there were earlier, before she went into a stall to clean the toilet seat a bulimic girl had soiled. Leaving the coins in the ashtray is a double-edged sword: it encourages forgetful ladies to leave something out of pity, but it's also a source of temptation to the kleptomaniacs who spend three times Mica's daily wage on breakfast and yet are capable of stealing a few pesos without the slightest pang of remorse.

Mica gazes dispassionately into the mirror, dropping the money into her apron pocket. Her supervisor had told her she was beautiful. That she wasn't cut out to be a cleaning lady. That she was smart. In fact, if she lost a little bit of weight…

*   *   *

Coffee with milk, a massage with a face pack, a chocolate-covered *polvorón*, a comfy chair, flour quesadillas, the latest romance of *Bianca* or *Jazmín*, which she had borrowed from her friend, a warm bath, a cup of camomile tea, the 9pm soap opera, sleeping straight through till morning… Mica had dreamed about it during her work hours, like a cat playing with a ball of wool. That was really what allowed her to keep going, and to put up with the rude women and her supervisor's sexual advances. With a bit of luck, Pedro would stay in Matamoros until next month. He hadn't sent any money on his last payday, and she probably wouldn't hear from him until he got paid again. His hangover would remind him of his vows to the Virgin of Guadalupe not to drink again and, feeling remorse, he wouldn't want to come home with empty pockets and whiskey breath. Soon he would call to tell her that his boss didn't pay him again, or that Dinero Express was closed, or that he had been robbed right after he cashed his check.

The hallway of her apartment building is dark as usual. The electricity is still out, despite all the calls to Señor Garralda's call-in show and the demonstrations in front of City Hall. At least there are no moths, Mica thinks, thanking God for the dead light bulbs. In her neighbor Juanita's shrubs, a couple of teenagers are having sex standing up. Mica sees the branches move and hears their panting breath. Looking through the dusty window, she sees colored lights flickering. The girl's mother must be ironing while watching TV. Juanita washes and irons others' clothes to feed her daughter and grandson. In the hallway some stray dogs sleep belly up, suffering from the heat. On the stoop a couple of kids take turns sniffing a can of Resistol 5000. At last Mica arrives at her front door. Before she goes inside, she picks up the canary cage that rests on the floor by the entrance. The bird rocks on its swing, its shiny black eyes looking at her with reproach.

"Forgive me, Marquesito. I'm late because the bus didn't come. I'll change your newspaper and water right away." The bird was a gift of repentance from Pedro after he hit her the first time. It was an argument over her cooking that had provoked her new husband's rage. They'd been married less than a month when he complained about the saltiness of the beans and the lack of variety in their menu. She reminded him that beans, tortillas, and eggs were the only things she could afford on his earnings. "When you bring me more money, then you can eat whatever you like."

Pedro started punching her, and in less than ten minutes she was lying in a pool of blood. She didn't pass out, but the pain spread all over her body until she was completely numb. She bled as if she'd been shot in the head: the scene looked like something out of a soap opera. Blood oozed from her broken lips and slid down her neck, forming a puddle under her head. Pedro ran away, fearing he had killed her. Juanita's daughter, who was around five and who used to go from house to house begging for cookies and candies, saw Mica lying on the floor and ran off, screaming that she'd seen a dead woman. Juanita called the ambulance from her corner store and later insisted that Mica file charges against her husband. Mica refused, but she remained grateful to Juanita. The two women became close friends, and if Mica had ever had children, Juanita would have been their godmother.

The next day, Pedro was full of remorse. "I swear, Mica. It won't ever happen again. I love you, *mamacita*. Forgive me. Forgive me. This is the only time. I swear I'll change. I don't know what got into me yesterday." Juanita, who had stopped by to check on her friend, slipped away before Mica forgave Pedro. The couple made up by trying to make a baby, an act of reconciliation that didn't bear fruit. What came a few hours after their noisy reunion was a beautiful cage with a white-breasted yellow canary inside. "Can you forgive me?" Pedro said, placing the cage in his wife's arms. "He looks like a marquis," Mica said, impressed with the bird's dignity. She named him *Marquesito* and took care of him as if he were her child. If Pedro had given her a canary every time he broke his promise, even thirty birdcages wouldn't have been enough. Fortunately, Pedro was never sorry again like the first time.

Now the bird trills in hunger. With the birdcage in her hand, Mica sighs and puts the key in the old lock of the door. A stink overwhelms her as soon as she enters the room. It's a mixture of rotten fruit, dirty underwear, stale meat, and unwashed flesh. A smell of pain, hate, and resentment. "Who's there?" Mica says, as she gropes her way in the dark. She has always tried to remain hopeful – without hope, she would have died long ago – and now she hopes to hear an unfamiliar voice, the voice of a thief who will stuff Mica's few belongings in a sack and then run off. But she knows it's really just Pedro.

"Is that you, Pedro?" She's answered only by a deep snoring sound. She remembers she has to wash the beans and put the clay pot on the stove. "Pedro?" Mica turns the light on and puts Marquesito's cage on the table. "First thing's first." The canary needs clean newspaper, birdseed, fresh water, and a blanket. "What next?" Mica sighs and looks around the small room she uses as kitchen, living room, and dining room. Empty beer bottles lie on the floor next to the couch. A half-empty bottle has dribbled its contents on the floor – the same floor that Mica had mopped that morning before she went to work. The yellowish liquid disappears under the couch, and a swarm of tiny ants marches along the sticky trail. She finds a muddy shoe on the couch (which Mica thinks is the most presentable piece of furniture in her house); a pair of pants rolled up like a giant condom near the bathroom door; and another shoe by a flowerpot. A newspaper is spread open on the metal table that she likes to call the dining room. She's glad she covered the tablecloth with a plastic sheet, because some kind of liquid is dripping from the table, forming a small pool on the floor. Mica follows a trail of footprints that disappears into the other room. She crosses the threshold, pushing aside the piece of translucent cloth separating the two rooms. There lies the mammoth, snoring in his drunken stupor, his ample belly moving up and down. The bristly hair on his arms and chest is drenched in sweat. A thick stream of saliva flows from the corner of his mouth onto the bedspread. The familiar sight of his body only repulses her. Mica imagines herself indulging in a foot massage, a warm bath, a chocolate-covered *polvorón*, tea, a soap opera, rest, spreading her wings and flying away. Again. She's scrubbed restrooms all day. She's battled against stingy, conceited women. Her feet are as big as motorboats. She deserves a rest and some pampering, but now she has more things to clean. Her monster of a husband lies on her bed, his limbs spread like a hideous starfish.

Mica's blood pressure rises like the mercury in a thermometer. In a few hours her husband will wake up expecting food on the table. If Mica doesn't comply with his demands, he'll use it as an excuse to beat her, and he won't let her complain about the money he has already spent, about the mess he made in the house, or about anything else. They've gone through it all a hundred times – the same old argument, the same old beating. He'll hit her and scream that she's useless, fat, and ugly, until his muscles are numb and he can no longer lift his arm. Then he'll make her stand up so he can see her face – her blood, her tears, her eyes filled with hate. He'll drop her into the chair, telling her he's not hungry anymore. He'll go outside for a walk until he reaches the bar.

Mica's lips twist with bitterness. She could wander the streets until he gets tired of waiting and leaves. She could go to her next-door neighbor's house and ask to stay there until Pedro is gone. Or she could run away, as she has done many times, to avoid the pain. But the humiliation is more difficult to hide from. It sticks to her skin like a blood-sucking leech, and when she tries to peel it off, a layer of her skin comes off, leaving a permanent mark on her. Of course, she could stay at home, eat, watch TV, wait for her husband to wake up, and let things take their usual course. She stands on the threshold, watching his chest heaving up and down. She tries to picture his ribs hidden underneath the thick layers of fat. Each time she inhales, the sharp smell of liquor fills her nostrils. "Then why did you marry him, Señora?" the social worker said, when Mica finally reported her husband's violence. Despite the dark bruises on her face and neck, the two police officers, with mocking laughter, told her to take off her blouse and skirt so they could see the alleged marks and judge whether a report was necessary. Mica remembers she left the police station with slow, heavy steps, feeling as if leeches were crawling all over her body.

Mica sits astride her husband and presses a pillow over his face. Time is a snail slowly crawling. Limbs moving in spasm, like a fish thrashing on dry land. Smothered moans. And then calm. When she removes the pillow, Mica sees dull eyes that don't stare back at her. Never again. Now she'll have to wash the sheets.

Periquita Shoes

Adán is quite certain she's the one. It always happens like this. If someone were to ask him, he would say another person had taken control of his body and acted without his consent. But no one would ever believe him, that's for sure.

The girl bends forward, waving the piece of bread in her hand. She presses her leather Periquita shoes against the bottom of the railing. Her dress reveals thin legs covered with scratches and mosquito bites. Dark strips of dirt remain on the backs of her knees, and the reddish dust of the cobblestones varnishes her brown skin. A little higher up, her purple nylon panties, with a weak elastic band, don't cover what makes him clench his fist around the wooden stick holding the balloons. A trio of coffee-colored ducks waddles over to the girl. She gets excited, jumping and laughing and stamping her feet, and he has to swallow hard through his dry, sandy throat.

He adjusts the balloons one last time, keeping the most expensive ones high on the stick, and the least expensive ones at the bottom, within the children's reach. The girl's image flickers before his eyes, blocking out the bodies of the Sunday afternoon shoppers. It plays out frame by frame: a woman of indefinable age, who could be her mother or grandmother, seizes the girl by the arm and the piece of bread falls on the grass. The ducks have multiplied, and they fight over it like crazed hyenas. Another frame: the woman moves her arms, her mouth gaping open and shut in front of the girl's sweat-stained face. Now a rear shot of the two walking away down the path of red hexagons, the woman dragging the girl. Cut. They're gone, or at least out of his sight.

His desire rises, blows up, a balloon reaching its limits. But there's no doubt – she's the one.

*   *   *

An involuntary jerk of his right arm makes him look away. His eyes burn, as if he hadn't blinked for minutes. He looks down: a head of spiky hair, a hand pulling on the string of a green frog balloon. It's an overgrown boy. The boy whimpers as he pulls on the string, but says nothing, giving the impression he's retarded.

"How much is the frog?" an elderly woman asks in a witchlike voice. The leather shoes, the dark knees and the purple nylon panties all disappear and before his eyes appears a yellowish face, a twisted mouth, and sagging cheeks, all framed by faded hair. The man's eyes slide down, taking in the pair of slack breasts and the belly that stretches out beneath them. He can't tell if she's pregnant or if it's the result of having given birth many times over the years. Grown-ups are disgusting. He wants her to go, to leave him alone. The woman's ugliness disturbs him. He knows her type: she'll haggle tirelessly until she gets the price she wants, and then she'll take hours to choose a balloon.

"I'm closed now," the balloon seller says and walks away, his dog in tow. He has a lot to do. First, he has to find her.

* * *

The girl's cry is high, clear, and sharp as a needle. It's louder than the joyful shriek of the magpies. It can be heard above the clamor of the fixed-route buses revving their engines at the bus stop, some fifty yards away; above the ringing of the church bells that announce the six-o'clock Mass; above the horn of the ice-cream cart pushed by the skinny old man. All these city noises, and still her cry rises high above them, threatening to draw attention to this isolated part of the park. Here, where the eucalyptuses grow so thick that few plants can flourish; here, in a place where only koala bears could thrive. A place with no swings, no bike or running trails, no benches for high-school sweethearts. The pines and poplars grow only in the most visited areas. Even the wild privets and cedars stand apart from the eucalyptuses, as if they were afraid of them. Around those white-barked trees stands an untamed row of shrubs covered with cobwebs: it's a place where only someone who likes bird shit on his head or the company of starving mosquitoes would dare to tread – or someone like him.

The girl can't be any older than seven, but malnutrition has kept her body small. Even so, she moves with unusual force – she kicks and cries, and tries to bite and scratch him. As if she weren't the one who tempted him, bending over in front of him to feed the ducks, showing him her dirty purple panties – which, he now discovers, have *Sunday* printed on them in a white cursive script. Surely she has the other six pairs at home, all in the same worn-out condition, each printed with a different day of the week. And it's actually Sunday. He imagines the girl doing her homework, writing meticulously in a small notebook. An orderly student. Poor, but hardworking. With a will to succeed, as people say.

Adán slaps her face a couple of times and sits on her, pinning her down. Beneath the worn-out dress, her ribs go up and down. He pants. His blows fail to shut her up. Adán places his palm over her mouth – her face is small enough to disappear inside his hand.

He bends to kiss her. She takes in the fetid air coming up from the man's stomach. He has to hold her thin neck, with its traces of filth, the small glands, the saliva struggling to reach her mouth, the air passages blocked. Her legs quiver out of desire to strike.

"Can't you see if you keep screaming, somebody will find us?"

She moans, the lowing of a frightened beast. Sparks are reflected in the dark marbles of her staring eyes, and her arms flap against the ground. Her small hands drive her fingernails into the dirt as she fights to twist free from his grasp. The ghostly wail of an ambulance on its way to the hospital drowns out all other sounds.

"If you shut up, I'll let you go. But if you scream one more time, I'll kill you."

The light brown bitch, now ailing, his faithful companion of ten years, looks up every so often, emerging from a daze to sniff the dirt near the wooden stick with the balloons. Her master leans over a small body that has stopped moving and is silent, no longer emitting a sound like the screeching of car tires.

The balloon seller kisses the girl's face, eyes, and mouth. She no longer tries to scream. It's been a long time since she started to defend herself, since she first realized she wasn't going to get a huge Hello Kitty balloon. She can't struggle anymore. Her strength slips away from her and she stares at the darkening sky. She sees the silhouette of a squirrel who is watching her from a low branch. She shuts her eyes tight and tries to send it a telepathic message: run, find a policeman, someone, it doesn't matter who, and ask for help. In the cartoons, everything seems so simple. The animals talk and think, and the superheroes have super powers. But the squirrel scurries away. No one can see her. No one can hear her. She can't talk. Three helpless monkeys.

The girl remembers the pig they made in school with a small balloon, glue, and shredded newspaper. Now she feels as if her body were made from that same material. The man on top of her smells like rotten broccoli. He rips her clothes off. He moans, hits her, pants, splits her in two, moves frenetically, makes horrific sounds, and hits her again. She swallows saliva for the last time and faints. Time stops. It's as if she has been thrown into an abyss, where, instead of falling, she floats in the air.

It gets light and the sun warms her skin. She can feel branches beneath her. She feels tiny legs crawling over her skin. The girl opens her eyes. Not a single cloud. Her body is alive. Without clothes, but alive. Full of pain, but alive. And tight on her feet, her Periquita shoes are still with her.

That First Time

He felt as if he had made love to a whale – and not just because it was a lot of work. Now he swayed in his hammock while counting the money he had "borrowed" from the woman. He'd promised to pay her back on the next date, but of course he wouldn't show up. He lay in the hammock like an albino monkey caught in a trap, or a giant mango raped by a rubber plant. He'd made off with a lot of cash, but he realized he wasn't as satisfied as before.

His parents had thought Antonio Azuara was a great name. They hoped the name would promise their son a bright future. But parents' expectations are as ephemeral as soap bubbles, and people always find a way to mess up your name. After that first time, everybody started calling him Tolito Ganzuara. His nickname wasn't going to be just an anecdote from his childhood: it seemed he had no choice but to live with it for the rest of his life.

Stretching out his hand, he picked a mango. He swallowed the fruit like an innocent child and flung the peel and pit over his shoulder. Not bothering to wipe his face, he decided to put the past behind him. He hopped off the hammock. Out of the tree's branches, he took an old cardboard box, which was still there by some miracle. As resolutely as a soldier putting on his boots, he pushed his long-nailed feet into the shiny rollerblades. His toenails were whitish and flaky, blighted by some unsightly fungus. His hair seemed to defy the wind as he slid away from his home – the space between the mango tree and the rubber plant. He had yet to learn that nothing is more persistent than memory.

He had lost the hymen of honesty before the age of ten. His parents asked themselves, again and again, where they'd gone wrong, flogging their consciences without getting an answer. He'd never had bad role models, and his family situation was never unstable – nothing had pushed him toward a life of crime. No, it was just one of those things. Even as a child, he'd been an incorrigible liar, and he took pleasure in coveting things that didn't belong to him.

After skating around the plaza, almost colliding with the nuns leaving the cathedral and the ten-cent whores going to five-o'clock Mass, he stopped in front of an ice-cream parlor. Several student couples were enjoying their ice cream. They lost their appetites completely when Don Tolito Ganzuara took a dirty handkerchief out of his jacket pocket and blew his nose. In front of him, righteous people entered the church. They looked like they obeyed every one of God's commandments, but in truth they took more pleasure in defying God than the devil himself. They soothed their consciences with pitiful alms and rigorous breast-beating.

The first time it happened, he was a bored twelve-year-old playing hooky from school. Robbing the Almighty was an unforgivable sin, but Tolito was so excited he would remember it for the rest of his life. He wasn't sorry for what he did. If he'd been looking for an incentive, he could have recalled the Robin Hood legend, or considered the notoriously extravagant lifestyles of certain church members – but when it came down to it, he needed no encouragement. After sitting through a long Sunday Mass as a devout Catholic, Tolito Ganzuara entered the confessional to tell the priest that he had committed the sin of theft. Muttering gibberish to himself, the priest with the onion-shaped body gave the smiling boy absolution. Tolita left the confessional and took a seat in a pew beside a few old women who were still bothering God with additional demands. He waited impatiently for them to finish their prayers.

Finally, when the old ladies had left and the altar boys were packing away the ritual tools, Tolito jumped to his feet and screamed, "Fire! Fire!" Taking advantage of his agile legs, the boy grabbed the alms basket and the golden chalice, ran out of the church and down the steps, and melted into the crowd. When he was sure no one was following him, he stopped to catch his breath. Admiring his loot, he realized he'd enjoyed what he had done. And if God knew everything, what was the point in hiding? After all, he'd asked for forgiveness in advance – and a truly merciful Lord would have no choice but to forgive. If He disapproved and wanted Tolito to stop what he was doing, He could use his infinite power to make it happen. With this reasoning in place, Tolita knew he was safe: he could become a professional thief without fearing God's wrath.

Now, the good times were gone forever. Boredom, party pooper of the human race, can ruin anyone's life. Tolito's robberies became more daring and sophisticated, but nothing could match the sensation of that first time. People think he's crazy, this weird-looking guy who rollerblades in circles around the plaza, shouting blasphemies against the church and hurling crude words at women out of his limited vocabulary. Nobody knows he's a kleptomaniac filled with sadness.

Stalin's Wife

Moira and I wait for Stalin's wife in a downtown café. We arrived on time, but we didn't expect her to be punctual: it's the mistress who must wait for the wife, not the other way around. I take a window seat so I can pretend to look outside while listening to the table next to mine. There, Moira takes out a pack of cigarettes and lights one without looking at me. I told her not to smoke because all the mistresses do and she shouldn't fall into this stereotype, but she just gave me an annoyed look and snorted. She's nervous – only I can tell.

The waitress comes over and offers me coffee and I accept. When she approaches the next table, Moira shoos her away, saying she's waiting for someone. She has that defiant look that single women sometimes adopt, a look men often seem to find irresistible. I wouldn't be surprised if some Don Juan offered to keep her company at any moment – it happens to women like her all the time. But not to women like me – when I sit in a café by myself, I prefer to become invisible. I'll stare intensely at the steam rising from my coffee cup, or make a point of checking my watch from time to time, as if I were waiting for a date.

Almost half an hour later, Stalin's wife appears. She turns her head, searching among the customers for someone who looks like a slut, I suppose. When they had talked on the phone and agreed to meet here, they didn't discuss how they would recognize one another – as if, having shared the same man's body for so long, they might know one another by scent alone. But maybe Moira has seen Stalin's wife before – perhaps she went through Stalin's wallet while he was taking a shower in their motel room and found a picture of her – because I see her stub out her cigarette and wave at Mrs. Stalin. Anyone would think she was experienced at this kind of thing.

Stalin's wife walks toward Moira with all the dignity afforded her by a piece of paper bearing the city's official seal. Like all wronged women, she walks with tight steps, her back erect. She's not horribly ugly, but she's far from beautiful: I can understand why her husband is seeing my friend, who, unlike his wife, doesn't look like a pug with slightly asymmetrical, bulging eyes. At least her hair flatters her: it's straight and shiny, and it cascades down to her waist like a model's hair in a shampoo commercial. But the poor woman has a nose like a *chile relleno,* long and broad. You can't help but notice it. Aside from that, she looks normal enough, perhaps a bit of a hippy, one of those women who have spent many years on a never-ending dissertation. She takes a seat in front of Moira and stares at her. Maybe she wants to know what it is about this woman that makes her husband want to sleep with her. Moira meets her gaze and lights another cigarette. She puffs smoke above her head, places her lipstick-stained cigarette on the edge of the ashtray, and spreads her hands on the table as if they were a peacock tail. Her nails are recently done – perfect.

"So?" Moira's voice is strong and beautiful, like a singer from the '80s. It never trails off. Sometimes I listen to her sing as she puts on makeup after her shower, leaning forward before the mirror, a towel just barely covering her. I didn't want her to come here and make a scene with this poor woman.

"Put yourself in her shoes," I told her in the car. "Your life turns to dust when you find out your husband is cheating."

"Well, her shoes must be really ugly," she answered. "She's not a material girl like me." Moira laughed as she said this: she always laughs when she wants to avoid something.

"I want you to stop seeing him," says Stalin's wife, a hint of melodrama in her voice.

Moira finishes her coffee and wipes her lips with a napkin. I don't know what they were expecting from this meeting – to measure one another, perhaps; to etch on their minds the other woman's image, and later lie awake at night comparing and contrasting each other using every possible parameter.

"If you want something, it's my treat," says Moira.

Stalin's wife tightens her mouth and remains silent. She's in a difficult situation, facing her husband's mistress, and she needs some kind of shield against her enemy. I flag down the waitress. She approaches meekly, a coffee pot in her hand, and Stalin's wife asks for a cup.

"I don't need your pity. I have a man to support me."

Moira laughs at this, but I can sense the falseness of her laughter. Cruelty is the best way to hide your fear, and she knows how to be cruel. The last time we drank together in our apartment, Moira told me how she suffered because of Stalin. She came near me, shaking, but when I leaned in to kiss her, she covered her mouth with her hand, disgusted. "When was the last time you brushed your teeth?" It was early morning, we were drunk, and it was completely unfair. I went to my room, curled up in my bed, and pretended to be the nonchalant, sleeping roommate.

"A man to support you? It's funny that a liberal like you boasts of being a kept woman. I thought left-wingers were feminists. You know, 'marriage is a bourgeois invention'…"

"Who told you I'm a leftist?"

"Stalin, of course. Do we know anyone else in common? Anyway, from what I've heard, you're actually the one who supports him." Moira's tone is childish, mocking.

Stalin's wife must be recreating in her mind a conversation between her husband and his lover where she's the main subject. The mixture of pride and humiliation she's feeling is a sensation I know only too well. The dessert cart passes my table and I order a slice of apple pie: I wish Stalin would go back to his wife, breaking Moira's heart into pieces like the pie crust against my fork. Maybe then she would realize I'm not there just to pay half the rent.

"Stalin and I are reconsidering our relationship. We'll start anew. He promised me he'd never see you again."

I see that she drinks her coffee black, without sugar. A wet mustache appears on her upper lip when she puts down her cup.

"I'm happy for you." Moira uncrosses her legs and plants her shoes firmly on the wooden floor. I know that her world is crumbling under her feet. Only a few days ago she told me she didn't understand why Stalin wasn't answering her e-mails, messages or calls. She began to gnaw her nails to the quick, but I dragged her to the manicurist to keep up appearances.

"But what's that got to do with me?" she says, in the most malicious tone I've ever heard.

"I want you to know this so you'll leave him alone."

"Then you should be talking to Stalin. He's the one who wants me."

Lying is the last resort of the cornered. Stalin's wife swallows hard and stares at her rival. I'm sure she wants to leap over the table, seize Moira by the neck, and squeeze out every particle her husband has left inside her, killing her slowly. But she can't, so she uses words. At first, she sounds awkward, like someone telling a child the facts of life. But as she rattles on, her voice grows stronger, and Moira's face darkens. Her body hardens, and I imagine her back is tense. She has become vulnerable, as fragile as marzipan.

Only I know how much she hates it when people make assumptions about her, putting her in a group of *people like you*, and calling her a *little bourgeois girl*. She can't stand those pedants who consider themselves above her just because they grew up poor.

And from the stories Stalin has told Moira – stories she poured out to me during our long evening chats – it sounds like the Stalins really have been less fortunate than Moira. They met in the Arts Faculty, in a class taught by a communist professor. They grew closer as they attended secret political meetings in abandoned places; went to lectures on books that seemed subversive to them, but could be found in any library; and shared the sin of eating a burger in a transnational franchise restaurant. His parents had been militant members of the Communist Party and that's why they named him Stalin. They thought the world was going to turn red, and nobody would raise an eyebrow when their son said his name. Her parents were middle-class people who had fallen on hard times, and that was a good enough reason for the young couple to unite against capitalism. The two had lived together for many years without getting married, but they finally tied the knot for practical reasons.

I'm sure the brand-name logos on her clothes weigh heavily on Moira. According to Stalin's wife, they represent the needle-pricked fingers of some third-world seamstress enslaved in a sweatshop. Moira's stomach begins to burn – it's her private education, the job in an air-conditioned office, the generous income that allows her to buy a whole new wardrobe every year and share an apartment in a good neighborhood with her best friend.

If this is a duel to the death, Moira is waving her sword weakly and losing a lot of blood. He could never really love her because her family has been more fortunate than his: resentment is the Berlin Wall between social classes.

"Stalin gave me all his passwords, access to his cell phone, everything I ask. We go everywhere together now. That's how I know he doesn't want you anymore – you, or any of the others."

A flat stone skids over the surface of a green, muddy lake. Stalin's wife smiles as she watches the pain forming ripples in Moira's eyes. "The loneliest place in the world is in Stalin's arms," she told me once during one of their many brief breakups. And now she must wonder whether she has been the only one to suffer inside those arms. There's no way to know if Stalin's wife is lying – and perhaps it doesn't matter. Why would Moira be the only woman to fall for this defenseless man, with his nervous breakdowns, his constant depressions, his poverty? For some women, pity is the strongest aphrodisiac. I signal the waitress for the check.

I don't know what Moira expected from all this, but what Stalin's wife wanted is clear: she wanted to get up triumphantly without paying her share, turning her husband's mistress into a pillar of salt on the chair. My friend would be left to look for some bourgeois man to marry so she could start making babies to drive everywhere in a minivan – the embodiment of everything Stalin despises. Moira will try to stifle a sigh, thinking about what she has lost, but she hasn't really lost anything. Even if I tell her this again and again, I know she will never understand it.

We walk together to the car in silence. It's already getting dark. I put my arm around Moira's shoulders and she, curling up against my body, lets me take her home.

Three Frosted Owls

Adriana pops a Listerine strip on her tongue and the acidic taste in her mouth diminishes a little. She sighs deeply and looks up. The mirror shows a thirty-year-old woman who appears five years younger, with a somewhat glassy look, but pretty. Pretty, despite the bleaching restroom light. Not bad, considering she's just thrown up. Attractive, even though she's the only one among her girlfriends who's single and not expecting her first or second child. Her skin is parched and dry – she has a vitamin deficiency, and she's too thin -- but all in all she's a good-looking woman. Still, the fear of becoming fat and ending up an old maid runs through her veins several times a day, like a cold, thick serum. If she applies mascara to her lashes, her fears recede for a while. When she puts lipstick on, her anemia is hardly noticeable. A touch of blusher under her cheekbones, and her self-assured, sensual look returns, a composed façade that won't crack until evening, when she's wrapped in her fabric-softener scented blankets: her brain tends to work extra hard when the room is dark.

Behind her, the cleaning woman makes a "tsk tsk" noise, spitting on Adriana's neck. Their eyes lock in the mirror. The woman points her chin at the lower part of Adriana's white blouse.

"Excuse me?" asks Adriana, staring at the woman's dyed yellow hair.

"You have a stain there, miss," she tells her, sounding pleased, like someone who's just helped an old blind woman with arthritis cross the street.

"Oh, thank you," Adriana answers, no hint of gratitude in her voice. She has orangish dots on the lower part of her blouse. She grabs a few paper towels and wipes brusquely at the fabric. She manages to turn the drops into a blurry cloud.

"That's going to make it harder to remove the stain. You'll just mess up. You should've used a pinch of bicarbonate and a few drops of lime juice."

"Thank you for the tip. I don't know why I didn't think of that. I should carry bicarbonate and limes in my purse at all times."

The woman must be immune to sarcasm and unable to read body language; she ignores Adriana's last comment and the shaking of her head. She dabs at the sweat on her forehead and ignores the bulimic girl who glares at her. She smiles, as if waiting for her to say something else.

Adriana snorts like a bull. She sounds like she might explode at any moment. The smell of shit floats out from the handicapped stall – whenever the women take a dump, they like to use the spacious handicapped cubicle, located at the far end of the room. "I hope she won't forget to flush," the cleaning woman prays.

"Forget about a tip, you busybody." Adriana crumples the paper towel into a ball and drops it on the floor with a touch of drama. She turns on her heels and walks out of the restroom, shaking her hips. Take that.

* * *

She walks back to her table, trying to control her expression. "Be calm and patient," her nanny always said. She taught Adriana not to show anger. Adriana had believed her nanny was a paragon of wisdom until she heard, on a call-in radio show, some guy named Kalimán giving the same advice to Piolín or Solín or whoever. It wasn't the first disappointment of her life – and certainly not the last – but it was one of the more memorable ones. She tucks her hair behind her ears, looks up, and meets the blue eyes of a flushed-faced foreigner. He grins at her, and Adriana gives him a flirtatious "Hi" in return, flashing a toothpaste-ad smile. He looks about thirty-five. Thirty-eight, tops. While he pays his bill, she pretends to look for something in her purse and checks out the firmness at the back of his khaki pants and his muscular arms under the blue shirt. Blond hair, earring-less ears, a strong profile with a natural nose. Out of the corner of her eye, Adriana makes out the grayish glitter of his American Express card sliding through the credit card machine. Bingo.

* * *

A waitress approaches, her tray loaded down with two large coffee pots. With catlike dexterity, she weaves around the children and wives who cluster near the cash register. At his window seat, Gabriel is hypnotized by the cleavage almost spilling out of her low-cut dress. She smiles at him as she pours coffee into his cup and puts packets of cream and artificial sweetener on the table. When he sees Adriana, he clears his throat and pretends to be interested in the three frosted owls on the window. He scratches them with his nail.

"Do they paint them by hand or use some kind of machine?" he asks, childlike. But he can't fool Adriana, who can revolve her head a full three-hundred-and-sixty degrees – like an owl.

"If you like cows, I can introduce you to one in the restroom. But don't treat me like shit, Gabriel." She collapses into the chair, shaking the table. The recently served coffee spills on Gabriel's pants.

"My new jacket!" The coffee seeps through the material, scalding his skin. The pain makes him resentful: they've been together so long, Adriana is starting to act like they're married – and she's taking the role of the angry, jealous spouse.

"Ooops, sorry! Tell your waitress girlfriend not to fill your cup to the brim. Look what happens."

"Stop, Adriana. What's wrong with you? You're paranoid."

She glares at him and grimaces. "Well, it didn't boost your ego, did it?" She sounds like a bad soap actress. "You want to bury your face in her bosom."

"Please, that's enough. I don't want to start the same old thing again. I've already told you – I only have eyes for you."

"That's odd, because I always catch you ogling other women."

"I have eyes. I can't stop looking, Adriana. But I don't know why you're acting this way."

"Oh, of course, you're so faithful. Why don't we ask your wife about that?"

"Shh, lower your voice. You know our case is different. I'm only married to her on paper – you're the one I love. I'm faithful to you, even if you don't believe me."

"Uh-huh. That's why you keep putting off your divorce." Adriana crosses her arms over her chest: no sex this afternoon. Not after this. Gabriel hasn't been getting any lately – but with two women in his life, he's been getting plenty of drama.

"I already told you, it's not as easy as it seems." Gabriel sounds like a teacher in front of a roomful of children. "My wife won't give me a divorce by mutual consent, and anything else is too much paperwork. But you know how much I want to be with you." He takes Adriana's hand; this always makes him seem believable.

She sighs and tries to keep a dignified face. She mustn't show desperation or lose her bearing. "It's getting harder and harder to believe you, Gabriel." She pretends to let her guard down just a little, so he'll do the same – a female mantis beguiling the male mantis into exposing his delicate neck. "You know I'm an independent woman. I'm modern. I don't need anyone to support me, nor am I one of those women who dream of getting married in church, dressed in white. But I love you and I want to live with you." When she softened her voice and fluttered her lashes, she was always able to get what she wanted from her father. Gabriel gives in too. A piece of cake.

"I love you too, sweetie. Let's go to the shopping mall right now. I'll buy you any ring you like." He flags down the waitress, gesturing for her to bring the check. He looks the very picture of the accomplished businessman, a man capable of keeping not only two but perhaps many women. The female mantis has devoured her mate's head.

"You look handsome today, my love. There's a jewelry store in the plaza, no?" A quick kiss on his lips; a recomposed face. The fine perfume of happiness floats in the air for a few seconds.

*   *   *

While Gabriel pays the bill, Adriana amuses herself at the buffet bar, admiring a large slice of pineapple carved into the shape of an owl and decorated with eyes of purple grapes, ears of melon wedges, and with a beak fashioned from a walnut. A cold, rough hand slips a note into her hand. Adriana turns quickly. The buxom waitress whispers to her while she loads fruit cocktails onto her tray: "The blond guy asked me to give you this. He speaks very good Spanish." Adriana nods silently and takes the piece of paper. The waitress winks to let her know they're in on it together. In ancient times, they used to kill the messenger to keep the secret from being passed on. How convenient.

"Okay, let's go," says Gabriel, tucking the receipt into his wallet. "What did the waitress want?"

"Nothing. She apologized for the provocative way she served coffee earlier. She saw that it caused our quarrel. But I told her you didn't even notice her. I gave her a tip."

"Oh my love. You're a real darling. That's why I adore you."

Adriana smiles and lets him take her arm. With her free hand, she slides the note into the pocket of her pants.

I'll Play the Piano
in a Wedding Dress

For Paloma Bauer

One more year to add to the twenty-nine I've already accumulated: today I turned thirty. I feel exactly the same today as I did yesterday. Andrei has left to spend the summer with his fiancée, my last Pap smear showed some abnormal cells, and now I have to make an appointment with my gynecologist.

I left the university just before five in the afternoon and stopped at a small organic market to buy a few things. I'm determined to change my habits, to eat healthier. Starting tomorrow, I'll swim before my sociology class. I'll stop smoking and eat more fruit and vegetables. The trees along the street are changing their leaves from green to yellow to red, and some have fallen on the ground. A few out-of-season cicadas chirp here and there.

I stop because my shoulders are sore from carrying so many books. After Andrei left, I read three or four books a week and ate whole packets of chocolate chip cookies dipped in coffee. I sigh and force myself to keep going. I've turned thirty, I'm alive, and I'm walking along a beautiful street in a college town. I still have my scholarship, and I'll finish my master's thesis very soon. Suddenly my bag breaks and a couple of cans of tomato soup roll down the sidewalk. Another link of sadness joins the others.

I know if I bend down to pick up the cans, I'll start crying and I won't be able to stop. I look around: no one is in the street, except for an orangish cat sharpening its claws against a tree. I can't afford to waste four dollars so, tears or no tears, I'd better go after the cans. On the sidewalk I see multi-colored chalk drawings: flowers, ladybugs, and hopscotch squares. It's been years since I was a happy child, drawing, jumping rope, and playing with my Slinky and my dolls. Now I'm independent and a student – the life I've always wanted – but I burst out crying in the middle of the block. The last forty or fifty yards to my apartment seem an infinite distance. How am I going to deal with these abnormal cells – and possible cervical cancer – alone?

The sky begins to cloud over and I know that I should forget about the soup and just hurry home. I lift my bag again and walk rapidly until the muscles in my legs force me to stop. By now it's started raining. I hug my bag and come around the stone-paved path that leads to my apartment, on the second floor of an old house. It'd be indistinguishable from any other building on the street, were it not for the fact that the landlady, who lives downstairs, has filled the entire garden with gnomes and frogs. I run through the figures, careful to dodge them because the rental agreement stipulates that if her tenants break any of the gnomes, she can evict them without notice. When I finish my master's degree and find a good job, the first thing I'll do is move out of this place.

It's dark inside and there's a faint smell of dampness in the air. I like my home this way, poorly lit. Andrei always teases me about it, saying that I must be at least partly Jewish because I'm stingy about electricity. "Then you can be with me," I'll answer, knowing full well he'll look down at the floor, grab my shoulders, and say, "You know I love you, but I can't marry a Gentile." And I will read from my part in the script, telling him, "We don't have to marry then." I want to torment him, to let him feel my pain. But he tells me the same thing over and over: "It's my duty to my parents. I promised them I'd marry a Jewish girl, give them Jewish grandchildren, and keep the family name alive." Maybe he thinks that if he keeps repeating himself, I'll understand and let him go. But why does he still sleep in my house? "Don't tell me you love me, Andrei. Obviously, you don't love me." Then I'll slam the door behind me and go out for a walk. Later, when I return home, I'll find him watching the news on TV with a beer in his hand, the lights off in my honor. He'll get up to receive me, say nothing, and begin to kiss me. We'll make love right there on the futon, with a CNN anchor giving the latest news on the Middle East conflict. Afterwards, Andrei will comment on what he sees on the TV and I'll caress his hair until we both fall asleep.

I put what's left in the bag on the kitchen table. I take out the kosher turkey ham and skim milk and put them away in the fridge. I go into the bathroom, pee in the dark, and then turn the light on to look at myself in the mirror. I think I can see more wrinkles around my eyes than before. I don't recognize myself. "I never used to be like this," I say aloud, as I imagine Andrei with his Jewish girlfriend. Are they seated on the living-room couch, with her parents interrogating him to see if he's a good prospect? Or are they together in the synagogue, holding each other's hand?

I should throw out all his belongings, starting with the razor resting on the edge of the sink. Or maybe I could use it to cut my veins. He'll come back and find me on the carpet in the TV room, a formless mass of dough, rotting. Then he'll see I'm a woman, Gentile or not, a woman whose body will decompose like any other. I take his razor and hold it up to my eyes. Andrei's beard is trapped between the blades. I don't want to cry again, so I put it back and leave the bathroom. I take three beers out of the fridge, sit down in front of the TV, and start drinking.

The last few months have been unbearable. I must be stronger than I think to have endured it for this long – or maybe I just have no dignity. I suppose it's the second. We live in the same place: he makes the breakfast and I do the dishes. And then, out of nowhere, a Jewish girl answers his ad on JewishSingles.com and they agree to meet. He says, "I'm going to Seattle or wherever to meet Sarah or whoever." Tears fill my eyes and he says again that he loves me but he can't marry me. Then I make a scene – shouts, maybe a broken coffee cup, and finally we make love until we almost lose our breath. The next morning, while I'm asleep, he packs his case. He kisses me and I hear him in my sleep telling me he'll be back in a couple of days. I turn away. When I hear the door shut, I press my face against his pillow and breathe in his scent. I feel miserable all morning; if I didn't have things to do, I'd stay in bed until he returned. In the end, he comes back and tells me Rachel or Abby is boring, he doesn't find her physically attractive, or they don't share the same religious beliefs. There's always something. Then it's my turn to be angry and Andrei's turn to look me in the eye and apologize until we go back to normal, at least for a little while. Later I'll say, "Maybe I should put up a profile on CatholicSingles.com."

Andrei pretends not to listen as he kisses me and takes my clothes off. "I don't want to end up an old maid if you're going to get married any day now." When we finish, still drunk from an orgasm, I'll continue: "You'll drive me crazy, Andrei." He'll keep quiet and let me talk, his face between my breasts. He's like a puppy who knows he did a bad thing when he chewed up the slipper. "And when I'm crazy, I'll play the piano in a wedding dress." He'll kiss me again: "You won't go crazy. You'll find someone who loves you very much."

I finish the last beer and change the channels. *Seinfeld* comes on and I remember how much we laugh together. Will I ever find anyone else who makes me feel this way? When he's not off looking for a Jewish wife, he's almost perfect. Once, a little drunk, he told me we could keep seeing each other after he got married. "That's not right. If you marry, you should be faithful to your wife," I told him. I never planned to be part of a love triangle. Still, there are times when I think I'd agree to anything Andrei wants, if only it would mean more time with him. But how am I supposed to play "the other woman"? I don't have a mysterious air about me, nor do I wear negligees or garter belts – I don't even wear makeup. I know it would never work. Andrei will spend the rest of the summer with his Jewish girlfriend, set a date for the wedding, and send me a postcard from their honeymoon. Then he'll settle in another city and we'll exchange e-mails less and less often, until he drifts completely out of my life.

I totter toward my room. I have to stop thinking about him. The best is to take, as the self-help books say, one day at a time. I promise myself I won't drink again until I'm in a stable relationship. If I keep drinking, I'll end up a pathetic alcoholic and nobody will ever love me. I'll call my gynecologist for an appointment first thing in the morning. I undress in the dark and drop my clothes on the floor. I'll start cleaning tomorrow. No dirty dish will stay in the sink for more than a day. I'll put a vase on the table and dust the books.

I lie down. My fingers touch Andrei's curly hair. His body shifts and he wakes. "I used my key," he says, hugging me.

"Shhh, I don't want you to tell me about your trip." He goes back to sleep and I hear his breathing. I stay awake with his arms around me. Maybe I won't go crazy — so long as I never buy a wedding dress.

Appointment with a Pig in the Library

Agatha Miller was married to Colonel Archibald Christie for fourteen years. When they divorced, she lost everything but Christie — *his last name must have been the best thing her husband had to offer. Divorce in those days... how brave! And with a daughter. She must have been one tough cookie.*

Señora Kikis checks her face and neck in the mirror. Tomorrow is her anniversary, but it's the thirtieth, not the fourteenth. Thirty years, a few wrinkles, and many more stretch marks. I bet Idelfonso won't remember it, she thinks. Her husband has a conveniently selective memory.

Oh, why didn't I divorce him sixteen years ago? Queta was already in middle school then — she could've handled it. She wouldn't be the first one among her girlfriends. Divorce is so common nowadays.

Kikis sucks in her belly and stretches the skin on her temples with her fingers. For a few seconds her crow's feet disappear. She had no wrinkles when she married Idelfonso. She was twenty, healthy, slender and happy. He was ten years her senior, handsome, the owner of Vizcaya Laboratories, the best business in the city, and the director of the Guadiana Park Association. That's where she met him. He was cutting a ceremonial ribbon in front of the duck pond, standing next to the governor, the mayor, and other important people.

I don't know what happened to him. He was so sweet to me. So young and handsome. Of good family.

If her husband doesn't bring her a bouquet of white roses and birds of paradise and invite her to dine at some fine restaurant this evening, she'll call Dr. Dreyfus in Houston and make an appointment for another facelift. Better yet, a facelift, liposuction, and collagen injections to her lips, all courtesy of the American Express card her better half gave her for emergency use.

Let's see if he ever forgets our anniversary again once the bill arrives.

Señora Kikis goes into the kitchen and finds Eufrosina leaning over the sink, struggling with the frying pans. She thinks of telling her maid to be careful with the expensive Teflon, but realizes she doesn't really care. Idelfonoso can buy her a new set. Surely he spends more on that slut, his secretary Margarita. No doubt about it, he's having an affair with her.

"Have you seen my Poirot cup? I want coffee."

"The one with the bald man's picture? It's in the dishwasher, Señora, but if you like, I'll bring you another cup."

"No. Take out my cup and wash it by hand. Then bring my coffee into the reading room. And remember, don't fill it right to the top. Three quarters, Eufrosina. Three quarters."

Doesn't she know I bought the cup in Torquay, Agatha Christie's birthplace? Why hasn't she washed it yet? Servants are impossible. They're brain dead, for goodness sake.

A few minutes later, Eufrosina comes in with a small tray. The steam wafts up from her favorite cup, the one bearing her favorite detective's profile. Señora Kikis signals for the girl to leave it on the table.

"Hasn't the mail come yet?"

"Yes, Señora, but it's for your husband."

"Why don't you bring it to me, girl? What concerns my husband concerns me too."

"Yes, Señora. Excuse me."

How stupid of her! It's impossible to find a smart housekeeper in Mexico. This one would incriminate herself before Miss Marple even arrived at the crime scene.

When she opens the glass door, the smell of mothballs and moldy old books fills her lungs. She pushes aside a five-volume set of English books, takes out a small bottle of cognac, and pours some into her cup. When she hears Eufrosina's footsteps approaching across the marble floor, Doña Kikis puts back the bottle and rearranges the books.

"What shall I read?"

"Excuse me, Señora?"

"Nothing. Leave the mail here and go back to your chores. I don't want to be disturbed."

"Yes, Señora. As you wish."

What would Poirot do? I know. He'd check my husband's activities. His expenses. Hmm, I wonder... here are his credit card bills. Let's see how he spends his money.

After glancing at the bills and sipping her coffee, Señora Kikis removes her glasses and sinks down into the couch. She didn't find anything interesting: just ATM withdrawals, payments for her new Mercedes, and charges from the shops she often goes to. There are also payments to some of the finest restaurants in the city, but she knows he wouldn't take his lover to those places – someone they know would see him and report his activities to her. There was a payment to the Flamingo Las Vegas for one week – but they went there together. Idelfonso probably took her there to distract her from something. Perhaps he was feeling guilty about being unfaithful? Apart from this, there was nothing incriminating.

But of course, whatever else he may be, he's no fool. He wouldn't use this credit card for his extramarital affair. Especially when he knows I could check the bill.

She thinks of Miss Marple. How would she go about solving this mystery? No, it's no mystery that her husband cheats on her – but how would Miss Marple find proof of the crime? She closes her eyes and revisits the twelve Miss Marple novels and twenty short stories. In all of them, she begins her investigation by finding parallels between the lives of the people of St. Mary Mead and what happens in the outside world.

Durango is a village, as they say – I must be able to find some kind of clue.

She needs to be methodical like Miss Marple. She tries to recall the plot of *Nemesis*. Instead, she remembers being ten years old, standing in front of a bookshelf at her grandparents' house, putting the Agatha Christie novel she'd just finished back on the shelf next to the others, all neatly lined up, all published by Editorial Molino. Her grandfather, a Spanish Republican, or rather an atheist, had them sent to him directly from Spain. He kept them in numerical order, and a few of the volumes were missing. Kikis couldn't wait for them to arrive.

"Señora, excuse me. May I bring you something else? I'm going shopping."

"Ay, Eufrosina. You almost gave me a heart attack."

"Pardon, Señora, but you always like me to tell you before I leave."

"But when I have migraines you must be more tactful, Eufrosina. Let's see, bring me another coffee, but use the same cup."

"Yes, Señora."

Señora Kikis closes her eyes again and sinks back into her chair. She begins counting inside her head.

Appointment with Death... *poison*. Five Little Pigs... *poison*. A Pocket Full of Rye... *poison*. Sparkling Cyanide... *poison*. Murder is Easy... *poison*. The Body in the Library... *the same*. *Poisoning was used in thirty-five of the sixty novels by Agatha Christie.*

When she was a child, reading mystery novels was her only hobby – or perhaps her only *vice*, as her mother liked to refer to it – besides taking secret sips from the anisette bottle her grandmother kept in the mahogany case under the console radio. She liked to go to her grandparents' house for books, for liquor, and for her mother's absence, in that particular order. Her maternal grandparents' house was a free daycare. Their bookshelves were always open, and the places where the bottles were kept were open secrets.

Is Eufrosina keeping something from me? And, if so, where would she hide it? In a bag under her mattress? No, maybe behind a picture of the Sacred Heart hanging above her bed. Or in the flasks of herbs she brings from her village. Maybe there.

Suddenly, Señora Kikis shivers as she did when she was a child. She recalls the sweet taste of anisette in her mouth and the way the alcohol made her feel lightheaded; the fragrance of the brand new book; the texture of the pages between her fingers; and the adrenaline surging through her veins when she knew she was about to join Miss Marple or Hercule Poirot in solving the crime. And then there was the sweet anguish of realizing that her mother would be back soon, looking for her all over the house, while she raced through the pages with a bottle of *rompope* in her hand, her eyes running over the words like a lizard scurrying through the desert.

But I must be missing something about the secretary. She has to be involved somehow. Ah, the photo from the Christmas dinner. There's Idelfonso with his employees, and she's right next to him. Let's put the photo on his desk. That's it, replace the photo of me and Quetita. Now he doesn't look like a family man.

Young Kikis wanted to finish one more page before her mother found her in her hiding place – in the pantry, in the closet beneath the stairs, in the fig tree, under the piano – and started shouting at her. Her mother's reprimands were always the same: the anisette had been filled up to the top of the monkey's face before and now it barely reached the tip of its tail; Kikis was on the path to alcoholism and perdition; and what was she doing anyway, reading those damned books that corrupted young minds? She should be doing embroidery, or helping in the kitchen, or reading about the lives of saints – not this filthy stuff about murderers and spinster detectives. When young Kikis said the novels belonged to her grandfather, her mother would lose her temper, jerking her head around like a puppet, strands of white hair coming loose from her bun. She would spit saliva and brandish the bottle. And Kikis would caress the glossy cover of the book, with its images that captivated her imagination, and guess who'd done it – the butler, the distant uncle, or the first wife.

Where is Quetita's letter to her father? The one where she says she hates him because he didn't let her go to Europe alone with her girlfriends. She wrote such horrible things – that she wished him dead, that she was ashamed to call him her father. It must be in a box somewhere. Idelfonso keeps everything, even the things that hurt him.

Eufrosina has gone out shopping, and the house is silent. As she rummages through the closets and drawers, Señora Kikis hears only the sound of her own footsteps on the carpet. She finds a triangular piece of plastic wrapper in the pocket of her husband's pants. Doña Kikis can't make out what's written on it, but she's sure it's a condom wrapper.

Of course, he wore these pants when he came home after nine in the evening, saying that the laboratories were being audited. Uh-huh. He can't fool me.

Señora Kikis examines Idelfinso's shirts, his pants, all his clothes. Of course, everything is clean. At least Eufrosina does that aspect of her job well. But his jackets? He wears them several times before they're cleaned. Ah, there it is – a long strand of blond hair on the lapel. She can't believe how careless he is. She thought he was smarter than this.

But Margarita has curly brown hair, and it's not as long as this. He's cheating on me with someone else? The horny bustard doesn't know when to stop. My God.

Kikis mechanically dials Idelfonso's work number. The phone rings three times before someone picks up.

"Vizcaya Laboratories. Good afternoon. This is Margarita."

"Idelfonso, please. It's his wife."

"Señora, he's not here. He left a while ago. He said he was going home."

Señora Kikis hears the front door open and hangs up quickly. Eufrosina has returned. She hears her moving around in the kitchen, preparing dinner. A few minutes later, Idelfonso comes home. As Señora Kikis receives his kiss on her forehead, she complains, as always, of a migraine. She asks how his day went, and he briefs her on the happenings in his office as he changes into something more comfortable.

He doesn't want his clothes to incriminate him. They must smell of another woman's perfume.

"Let's eat, Kikis."

"Yes, my love, let's go. Eufrosina should have dinner ready by now."

They go down the stairs together, Señora Kikis linking her arm through his. Scarlet O'Hara and Rhett Butler.

"Do you know what day tomorrow is?"

"Last day to file taxes? Don't worry, Margarita took care of everything."

Señora Kikis fakes her best smile, pleased she was right.

I knew it. Ay, my love. Why do you make me do this?

The dinner goes well. When he finishes eating, Idelfonso retires to the library to look over some bills for the laboratories. Señora Kikis sends Eufrosina to the drugstore for more migraine pills.

"The dishes can wait till tomorrow; my headache, no."

Señora Kikis pours cognac into her Poirot cup. In a second cup, a simple, cream-colored one, she pours coffee over the blue powder and watches the foam disappear. Then she arranges several MacMa cookies in a fan on the plate and sets out containers of sugar and cream. Finally, she places a teaspoon on the tray with the ornamental handles.

The library door creaks when Señora Kikis pushes it open with her foot. She enters the room, tray in her hands, and Don Idelfonso raises his eyes from his documents and smiles. She sets the tray down on the table, takes a seat on the couch in front of him, and crosses one leg over the other.

"Idel, sweetheart. Will you join me for some coffee?"

A Model Kit

Your guest stares back at you with fear – or so you assume, though you've never experienced fear yourself, and you can't be certain that this is what it looks like. Waldteufel's *Skaters' Waltz* drifts in the air, echoing through the apartment. "The eyes are the window to the soul," say certain naïve romantics. And now those eyes look like they're about to pop out and fly across the room. Or perhaps they're learning to speak: first they speak in silence, and then they scream, ripping the air. They flash with a primitive light, like the eyes of a caveman who knows he's about to be devoured by a wild beast.

Ah, you always get lost in digressions. Fear shines in her eyes every time you draw the knife closer to her face. She struggles to scream under her gag. "Hope dies last." It's hard to believe, but this corny old saying is true – and so fitting for the occasion. Still, you know her hope is short-lived: the women fall into a stupor once they realize there is no way out. Some pray for a quick death. This one thrashes about like a fish struggling to survive out of water. She's trying to loosen the rope tying her limbs to the chair. You give her a polite smile – you behave like a gentleman under all circumstances – and ask if she has seen *Un chien andalou*. She shakes her head. Just as I predicted, you think. How could someone like her possibly appreciate Buñuel's masterpiece? You slide the blade of your knife across her left eyeball, which splits open like a ripe pomegranate. Then you remove it from its socket and rinse the knife with soapy water in a container.

You make a cup of apple tea with cinnamon while you leaf through the pages of the local paper. Bar brawls, bodies hacked to pieces with machetes, so-called crimes of passion, drug traffickers settling scores, cops-and-robbers shootouts, territorial and religious wars fueled by young, suicidal idiots. Adolescents who pepper-spray old folks and rob them. Everything seems vulgar, in poor taste. Disgusted, you sip your tea, push aside the newspaper, and stare at the girl who sits across from you.

"What could be more tasteless than to kill an old man who already looks like a corpse? Nobody appreciates a good murder anymore," you tell her, a touch of dissatisfaction in your voice.

She returns your gaze with her only eye, but she no longer tries to escape. Has her hope drained away, like the watery remains of her eye that now brush lightly against her chest, dangling from threads of whitish nerves? You offer her tea and butter cookies, but she shakes her head again. So much for trying to be nice.

Just to make small talk – after all, you're the host and there's no hurry – you assure her that the proposal you made at the mall still stands. You tell her once more that she's young and beautiful – women like to hear this again and again, regardless of the circumstances – and an ideal model for your next painting. And it's true. You've never lied. Lying is for those beneath you. You tell her she won't get paid, but she will be immortalized in your painting. And isn't that what artists and models want? Recognition. Those poor souls are starving for recognition and self-esteem. This painting, you promise, will make her famous. The two of you will benefit from this brief relationship. Of course, her fame will come only after her death, but she doesn't need to know that right now. You just tell her that you'll need more than makeup and lighting to create the perfect image. But this shouldn't be any problem for you.

You step into the living room to change the music. You think Saint-Saëns's *Danse Macabre* will provide you with more inspiration. Your steps make muffled sounds on the brown carpet. You serve yourself a glass of Chianti and take it with you to the study, where you check that the easel and paint are ready and in place. The chessboard is covered with a plastic sheet, but you're a cautious man, and you spread a large sheet of brown paper over the top. You put on a transparent raincoat and return to the kitchen. She jumps, startled by your entrance. You tell her everything is ready and help her get up from the chair. Again, as she did a few moments ago, your guest offers resistance. You ask her if she wants to lose another part of her body, and she stops fighting. She's not so stupid after all.

It amazes you that she still believes you'll feel compassion for her and let her go. Compassion is one of those empty words that means nothing to you – or to anyone else, judging from what you see on the street and read about in the international section of the daily newspaper. You are what you are – an artist – and you're passionate and egocentric enough to do what it takes to realize your artistic vision. Unlike all the others, you don't seek to justify your actions as the consequence of some past trauma – and you're certainly not one of those hypocrites who invoke 'human nature' as a mask to hide behind while doing evil.

Today you feel inspired by Walter Sickert: late-nineteenth-century painting has always been your favorite. There's something

almost endearing about the way fear captivates the world at the end
of every century. Humans are so predictable, you think. Not much
more than a century separates Sickert from you, the painter of the
new millennium. However, his work still has an impressive validity.
You're convinced that Sickert was Jack the Ripper – who but the
killer himself could have captured the crimes so brilliantly on
canvas? Even a painter of genius and imagination couldn't have
dreamed up the positions of the bodies merely from reading the
accounts in the newspapers. And when you compared the photos
in the police archives with Sickert's paintings, you found a number
of similarities between them. But you keep this theory to yourself,
because these subjects make people uncomfortable. Even the art
critics would fail to understand your admiration for Sickert and his
work.

Now, as you bring one of his paintings to mind, you grab a
knife from the worktable and head toward your guest. She blinks
her only eye, perhaps sensing your next move. The remains of her
other eye have dried in the bloody socket, resembling a kind of
coral reef. You apologize for not having a refined couch on which
to lay her body, à la some nineteenth-century model who reclines
on a chaise longue with a sweet half-smile on her face. You order
her to lie down on the sheet of brown paper. You're about to cut
off her head, but change your mind at the last minute. Everyone
knows you can't plan a work of art as if it were a boring party or
the construction of a building. Crime, like any other form of
artistic expression, is liable to the whim of the artist, the
circumstances of his subject. You take a scalpel and make a neat cut
through her blouse as you draw the blade along her stomach. You
could strip her naked, but you've always enjoyed watching the
blood seep through the clothes, gradually darkening the material.
On this occasion, her blouse is white and will give greater contrast,
enhancing the visual effect.

You don't have a surgeon's knowledge of anatomy, but practice has made you skillful. You make a wide, precise cut, and the skin splits open more easily than you expected. A layer of fat spreads underneath, but you have no problem dealing with it. Going deeper, you come to the transparent cover that provides the last flimsy protection for the organs. By this time the woman's primal shriek has died away into a soft moan, as if she is trying to comfort herself. You don't know why, but you suddenly recall the countless cats and dogs you tortured and cut up when you were a boy. A sharp cry brings you back to the present and you start separating her internal organs. You stretch her stomach until you can lift it up and place it on one side of her body, next to her hips. You do the same with the liver and kidneys, making a bloody circle around the woman's gaping torso.

Before you forget, you slice off her left nipple – you need it for your box of souvenirs. You'd like to start collecting eyeballs – it has recently occurred to you that a large fishbowl filled with eyes would be wonderful – but you're reluctant to abandon your impressive nipple collection. Besides, it requires considerable time and care to keep eyeballs wet and shiny.

You put the small keepsake in the box along with the others, pausing to consider the incredible variety; this new one, for instance, is small and pink, with no areola. Then you return to your model and begin to slice open her chest. Inside, you discover a pair of fake breasts. How did you miss the scars beneath her breasts, the crude and revolting proof that a modern Frankenstein had been at work on this miserable body? You throw away the silicon sacks and tuck a round piece of meat from her belly into each empty pouch. Then you take a moment to finish your glass of Chianti.

Her clothes are soaked with blood, like the paper and oilcloth you put down to protect the floor. The woman seems to have fallen into drowsiness, and the pulse in her neck is faint. You decide to give your beautiful model a purple necklace, and make a deep incision to her throat, severing the artery. You're surprised by the weak splash of blood that comes out – the abdominal bleeding must have lowered her blood pressure. You grab her thin intestine and drape it across her neck like a gray stole. Then you strip her naked from the waist down, exposing her smooth, tanned legs. You run your hands up and down her legs, not with lust, but rather like a sculptor caressing a block of virgin stone. Then you pour yourself more red wine.

With the glass in your hand, you gaze at your guest's vulva for several minutes. You find it beautiful, but defiant. With a new scalpel you cut off her external labia. Now her clitoris, out in the open, looks like a vulnerable king, his shoulders draped in a carmine-colored robe. Then you remove all the hair – dark, thick, vulgar – from those lips and place them diagonally on the woman's mouth, which she has cut trying to free herself from the gag. You now realize she's already dead and curse yourself for having missed it. The moment of death is beautiful and indescribable, almost mystic, and you try to observe it in all your victims. You want to witness some kind of transformation, a sign, maybe even catch a glimpse of the soul leaving the body. With her vulva on her mouth, your model reminds you of a Carlos Fuentes story, the one where the lips of a Tamayo painting stick out from the canvas and eventually come loose.

An image assails your mind. A sudden impulse makes you grab a saw and amputate all four limbs – you need more material to work with. Sawing through bone should be difficult, but her limbs come off easily. Once you have the four pieces, you cut through them once more at the elbows and knees. Then you arrange the limbs as if each part is bent. You have created something similar to the Aztec moon goddess Coyolxauhqui, with a hint of Sickert and a touch of Fuentes. No doubt this type of primal collage will inspire a new genre.

You own an excellent Polaroid camera, a digital video recorder, and other high-tech accessories, but only you, your paintbrush and the canvas can really capture the beauty and the emotion of this scene. For you, this is the most expressive medium, and each new work reveals more about you than you'd like.

Disposing of the body is routine, just like washing the brushes and other utensils. True, you have to crush the skull, cut the body into smaller pieces, wrap all the pieces in brown paper, and stuff them in a large garbage bag. And you must ensure that not a single drop of blood is left. You have to roll up all the paper on the floor and put it in another black garbage bag. Then there's the quick trip to the outskirts of the city, one of those waste dumps, where someone once bothered to put up a sign that reads "Please Do Not Litter." It's the perfect place to dispose of the leftovers from your most recent masterwork.

Even though you often complain about living in a primitive country like yours, at times like this it comforts you to know that no group of forensic detectives will ever link your model's body to you – they won't even manage to find it.

A few weeks have passed since your painting debuted at a museum in Mexico City. As you sip your latte in the Café de Artistas, your colleague reads aloud from a review of your most recent masterpiece:

"*...his painting was well received by his feminist supporters, who stated that the work was a raw representation of a modern woman who is forced to live in a brutal and chauvinistic society, a society in which she feels torn between her professional ambition and her desire for motherhood. The subject is depicted with exposed bowels – a woman literally ripped apart by her self-loathing, and by the impossible standards imposed on her by the mass media. And yet, through it all, she must pretend to be satisfied and content, as is shown by the artist's superb rendering of the false smile on her lips...*"

You can't help smiling at the irony. You gulp down your coffee, push the empty mug to the middle of the table, and sigh. "My work has been misinterpreted once again. We artists can be so hard to understand."

To Adorn the Saints

"If you don't find a husband, you'll be left to adorn the saints."
— Mexican proverb

In the streets of San Cordelio de Cocoyótl, orange peel, tamale leaves, dust, and people jostle rhythmically against the wind. It's the annual feast day of the town's patron saint, and the villagers have gathered to celebrate with singing, dancing, and the spirited practice of a few of the deadly sins. Suddenly, in the bell tower, a woman appears. The men in the church courtyard raise their eyes and see Ludivina Castañón, naked and dangling by her hands from the rope of the bell, her breasts swaying to the rhythm of the clapper. The noises of the fiesta fade one by one, like a saucepan of popcorn that gradually stops popping, kernel by kernel, until there is silence. The men urinating suspend their golden trickles, frozen in a perfect arch from their penises to the ground. Some of them lose their aim and wet their neighbors. The dancers in the courtyard take off their masks in surprise, and their bodies turn into motionless figurines. The crybabies stop their resentful sniffling, wipe their snotty noses with the backs of their hands, and become quiet. The ardent solitary candle intensifies its flame, and even the eyes of the adorned icon seem to widen with interest. In a moment, all eyes are on the bell tower. Jaws drop, pupils marvel, imaginations run wild.

Ludivina Castañón keeps swinging under the bell, naked as a fish, the queen of the fiesta, of the church, of the whole village. From below, the celebrants can't take delight in the minute details. They can't see the texture of her freckled skin, spotted and sweet-smelling like the peel of a ripe banana. Nor can they appreciate the delicacy of her beehive hairdo, full of hairspray, so vertical and fantastic. And even more difficult to discern is the virginity that Ludivina Castañón has had to painfully endure in every pore, in every cell of her body, for many years.

In the village, they had always suspected that Ludivina Castañón had a touch of madness. There even exists the myth that in her boarding house, exclusively for men, the mature single lady liked to play the dining-room piano in her birthday suit when her tenants came downstairs for their afternoon snack. But it was nothing more than a rumor, and no man in the village could testify with absolute certainty to Ludivina's alleged exhibitionism. On the other hand, the women saw Ludivina at Mass each day, receiving Holy Communion, and they could attest to her piety. She was always dressed austerely and modestly, clutching a rosary and the Bible in her hands. No one had the audacity to speak ill of her in public, unless their gossip could be passed off as sympathetic commentary: "Poor Ludi, so lonely and helpless, with no man to look after her."

But this is a day unlike any other, and there is no whispering behind anyone's back. Here she is, in front of the whole village, exposing her fallen breasts, her smooth hips, and her pubes, an unspoiled forest, while the bell tolls wildly. The women's hands flutter back and forth, first covering their children's eyes and then their husbands'. The most avid stare certainly belongs to Catarino, the sexton, who, by the way, doesn't believe that his role as the priest's assistant necessarily entails a life of celibacy. He has a varied "menu" that includes the sheep and hens from the corral, and the ladies in the red light district, who give him a discount once in a while. He is a chubby, generous man, and when he at last looks away, crossing himself, he is overcome by anguish. How many times has he undressed Ludivina Castañón with his eyes when she got in line to receive Holy Communion! It's true, he has undressed in his mind all of the women who attend Mass. Still, Catarino suspects that Ludivina's madness is a divine punishment for his carnal thoughts. "Mea culpa. Mea culpa," he cries, striking his brown and hairless chest.

Suddenly, silence returns to the village. Confident that the entire town is watching her, Ludivina has stopped pulling the rope of the bell tower. The old men are about to burst into speculation about her motive. The women can't resist exchanging shocked and caustic critiques of Ludivina's body. The younger men want to shout something vulgar – anything – because their simple natures don't inspire them to do anything else in a situation like this. The priest assumes responsibility for the matter – after all, Ludivina is in the bell tower of *his* church and is a member of *his* flock. He whispers a few words to an altar boy – the one referred to by the villagers as 'the mental defective' – and the boy runs off toward the church. He returns a few minutes later with the news that the naked woman has shut the belfry door and bolted herself inside the tower.

Before someone can mutter a curse or come up with a brilliant plan to remove Ludivina Castañón from her confinement, something happens: she appears at the tower window, where people can take a better look at her. Between her breasts, which are like two giant pink-nosed caterpillars hanging over her belly, she holds a brown-feathered pigeon. She kisses its oval head and then releases it into the air. The creature lands gracefully on the sexton's shoulder, as if guided there by San Jorge himself. Catarino is about to lift the bird down and take it home – perhaps he wishes to save it for a lonely moment when the sheep aren't around – when someone notices the piece of paper tied around its leg. "It's a carrier pigeon," says Doña Cococha, snatching the unhappy bird from the unhappy sexton. By the authority vested in him by God and none other than the Pope himself, Father Girasol opens the sheet of paper, adjusts his glasses, and reads the note aloud, as if he were giving one of his best sermons:

I'm my own hostage. I'll stay locked up here until the following conditions are met:

1. *Send a man to the bell tower. He must be young and attractive. At the very least, he must have serviceable equipment and be able to deliver the goods.*

2. *The man must stay with me for at least one night and must be at my complete disposal.*

3. *The man must bring a garnish of strawberries and guavas, as well as a bottle of red wine and a pizza with mushrooms.*

4. *If someone comes to rescue me without the man I desire, or if the man doesn't turn up within the next three hours, I swear I'll jump from the window and you, the people of San Cordelio de Cocoyótl, will be responsible for my death.*

> *Yours sincerely,*
> *Ludivina Castañón*

The married women forcefully but discretely squeeze their husbands' arms so that no one will offer himself as a volunteer. The adolescent boys are itching with raging hormones and recently awakened lust, but not one of them says a word: Ludivina, the virginal Señorita Castañón, couldn't be further from the sex goddess they've been dreaming of. The priest excuses himself by default, while the old men are ruled out, sadly, by the sobering toll gravity has taken on their virility. It all seems to point to Catarino, the sexton – he's the only choice! Father Girasol forgives his sin in advance – God will turn a blind eye when a pious man is on a mission to save a life – but privately resolves that the two will later become man and wife.

The sexton sighs, feigning resignation. "I'll just have to sacrifice myself," he mutters. He knows very well that when all's said and done, it would be nice for him to have a female companion of his own species, just for a change. A few of the women run to get the wine and fruits, and someone orders a pizza by telephone – no peculiar feat these days. With the free market and the global economy, modernization has reached even this tiny village: the dirt roads are lined with pizza franchises, and telephone companies fight for the few inhabitants' paltry business.

In the midst of the uproar, no one remembers the patron saint of San Cordelio de Cocoyótl. The saint's icon, dressed in fine clothes and wearing a gold-plated crown, sheds a tiny teardrop: from now on there will be no one to adorn him.

A Sip of Light

The usual shadows of the restaurant have grown darker. The unseasonal rain lashes against the window next to her table. Milena has asked for a second cup of coffee. She pours cream into her cup and glances out the window, where the raindrops are bouncing off the pavement. Men and women flee from the downpour, their shoes floundering in the countless small puddles. Passersby improvise raincoats out of large plastic bags, and the students cover their heads with books and backpacks. Mothers hurry home, dragging small children who seem to fly behind them like paper kites. Old people hold onto their hats with one hand and their wobbling walking sticks with the other. In a few minutes everyone is gone, except for a few beggars and the stray yellow dogs that hide under the cornices. In the distance she sees the dark sky, a dirty blue flannel, occasionally broken apart by bright white lines of lightning. Milena opens the magazine in front of her and tries to concentrate on a story. As she turns and flags down the waitress for some sugar substitute, she notices a couple a few tables away. With a desperate look in her eyes, the woman is attacking a pile of enchiladas, her cutlery clanking against the plate. She pretends to listen to her companion, who sips his beer in between sentences, swallows a piece of roast beef, and carries on his endless chatter.

*   *   *

Her aunt and uncle in the city lived in the biggest house Milena had ever seen. The spacious bedrooms, painted in bright, fresh colors, had large windows framed by soft curtains swaying in the breeze. The living and dining rooms looked like furniture displays in some classy department store. The sofas and chairs were upholstered in fabric that matched the curtains. Lamps, paintings, porcelain figures, cut-glass ashtrays – everything seemed to come from the same catalog. Outside, the view was beautiful, and the garden shone brightly in the afternoon light. The walls bordering the garden were covered with vines, and flowering shrubs guarded the entrance to the orchard. In the middle of the lawn, a plum tree brimming with fruit and a peach tree in blossom reigned proudly over the other trees. It was a beautiful residence, and it took Milena a while to realize that things were not as sunny and welcoming as they initially appeared.

Her mother thought it best for Milena to study in the city, where "everything is civilized and modern." She decided to send Milena to live with her brother and his wife, who gladly offered to take the girl in for as long as necessary. When they first went to her uncle's house, Milena was five, with her hair in pigtails and her dark eyes set against her pale skin like dominos. Her mother, older and heavier, was certain that she was doing the best thing for her child, and she eagerly approved of everything about the place that was to become her daughter's new home. Seated on a big sofa in the living room, Milena felt as insignificant as the specks of dust that had gathered on the glass of the main table.

Her aunt and uncle seemed anxious to give them a tour of the house. Milena's bedroom had already been prepared. The bedspread was printed with blond, curly-headed dolls, and a brown teddy bear rested on the pillow. The entire closet had been emptied for her, and a small pinewood desk was waiting for her school materials.

"Ah, Milena, darling. You'll be the daughter we never had," her aunt said, wrapping her stout arms around her. Milena felt the woman's large breasts pressing against her face. Her aunt smelled like chlorine, onions, and pepper.

*   *   *

It's not the restaurant that has darkened, but her eyes. When the waitress brings over the small blue packets for sweetening her coffee, Milena sees only a gray silhouette: she can't make out the horizontal rainbow stripes on the waitress's skirt, nor the V-shaped purple bib on her white blouse. She turns back to the window and glances outside, making sure she's still in the same place. The streets look the same, and the magazine stand on the corner hasn't disappeared. The rain is falling steadily. Pools of muddy water join together, timidly forming coffee-colored puddles, which remain undisturbed until tires splash through them. A carton of French fries and scraps of roasted corn drift down a small river that runs along the street toward the drain.

Two tables away, the couple has finished eating. They order coffees and Milena fixes her eyes on them again. The woman plays with her spoon, tapping it against her cup while pretending to pay attention to her companion. But she too looks outside from time to time, to a place beyond this chattering man. The words pour from his mouth like squid ink, damp and thick, viscous and staining, plunging everything into total darkness.

*   *   *

At first, her mother came to visit her once a month, and she took an interest in Milena's progress at the elementary school. But after that first year, when Milena turned six, she came less and less often, and finally she stopped visiting altogether. Milena was allowed to spend the summer in the country with her mother and father, but family tradition dictated that Christmas be spent at her uncle's house, and this was the only time her parents visited her in the city. When Milena realized she would only see her mother twice a year, the bitter fact of her abandonment planted itself in her mind like a nest of rats in a cupboard, and she decided to disappear.

The first time, her aunt looked for her for hours, shouting her name with increasing desperation. Milena woke after a while and emerged sleepily from the closet she'd been hiding in. When she did, her aunt and uncle scolded her. How dare she frighten them like that? Her aunt, with tears in her eyes, gave her a loud, painful slap. When her aunt left the room, her uncle tried to hug her, rubbing her back as if warming her. An intense chill, like an icy scorpion creeping down her spine, traveled over Milena's back.

Despite the scolding she received, Milena became fond of remaining still, like a clay toad, inside the closet. She would stay in there for hours on end. The smell of clean linen reminded her of her mother and eased her longing for home. The silence cuddled her softly, putting her in a state of mental coma: her mind stopped racing and she could finally rest. She got so used to the darkness that the world outside the closet, with its light and colors, caused her pain. And her bedroom offered no sanctuary – the darkness there was different, colder and somehow threatening. She tried to take comfort in the smell of the sheets, but it wasn't the same. Once they were placed on the bed, they lost the scent she associated with her mother and got soiled with sweat, sweat that wasn't hers.

*   *   *

Traversing her pale forehead, a bead of sweat seeps into her eye, like a teardrop that has somehow traveled back in time. And then more beads gather and cover her forehead, a bunch of salty grapes. An immense uneasiness invades her, a violent takeover of her whole body by the brigades of utter sadness. Dizzy, Milena walks slowly toward the restroom. She doesn't bother to take her purse with her or finish her coffee, which will be cold by the time she comes back. She's not in a hurry, she just needs to leave, to escape the scene for a moment. The route seems arduous, and she barely squeezes through the small spaces between the chairs and tables in the restaurant. Milena runs both hands through her hair, her eyes fixed ahead, not daring to look at the people dining.

In the restroom, she places her hands flat on the edge of the sink and considers her reflection in the mirror. A woman putting on her makeup looks at her somewhat scornfully. Milena, sweaty, disheveled and watery-eyed, shivers softly, visibly shaken. The woman seems torn between ignoring her and faking concern. In the end, she takes one more quick glance in the mirror, stuffs her cosmetics in her purse, and walks out without saying a word, leaving Milena alone.

Milena knows she's not the same as she was before. She's no longer the girl who took refuge in the closet for a whole afternoon – but when she looks in the restroom mirror, she sees herself frozen in anguish, a child once more. She shakes her head to dislodge the image. She's no longer a child. She has grown tall, like a plant that somehow thrives in shade. And she is still alive.

*   *   *

It all began with an innocent tickling game. Her uncle would hug her from behind and draw her onto his lap. Later, it evolved into something more. Little by little his hands ventured further up her legs and under her dress, as he chose to interpret her desperate screams as giggles and laughter. It always happened at lunchtime, while her aunt was fixing food in the kitchen. That was when her uncle always wanted to spend time in the TV room "with his favorite niece." One day, during the daily torment, her uncle slipped his fingers into Milena's pink panties. There was no more tickling, only an icy silence that left her still and stunned. Her body, not her mind, felt his thick, sweaty fingers pressing and rubbing her vulva. The man's rough, smothered breathing filled the room. Now he licked his finger and put it into a part of her body Milena didn't know existed. Suddenly everything seemed to sink under a pressing silence, as if all motion had turned into a postcard, frozen. His left hand rubbed the crotch of his pants. When an ice floe of pain went through her, her uncle moaned like a wounded animal and then stopped. Milena stayed on his lap for a few minutes, staring at him blankly, unable to move. When her aunt called from downstairs to tell them that lunch was ready, she ran to her bedroom and went into the closet. She wrapped herself in a wool sweater, but she couldn't stop trembling. Nor could she listen to her uncle telling his wife that the girl had decided to take a nap and would eat later.

* * *

She stays in the cubicle for several minutes, crying softly behind the closed door, just as she had done in the closet. Then she gathers her courage and steps out. She washes her face with care, wets her hair, ties it up in a ponytail, and tidies herself up as much as possible. The only thing she can't remedy is the reddish color of her eyes – that, and the infinite sadness that seizes her throat. There is a huge void there, an old, familiar hunger. Several women – the kind that always travel in a flock – come into the restroom, chattering and laughing together. They place themselves in front of the sinks next to Milena, and jostle her for a piece of the mirror, a piece of their own image.

What if she were to tell them everything? Would they stop worrying about finding a maid, catching an end-of-season sale at the Palacio de Hierro department store, holding on to their husbands against the odds? Would they stop shoving her and pause to think for a moment, putting down their powder puffs and their mascara wands? Probably not. Neither her aunt nor her mother had listened to her. One afternoon she found her aunt alone in the kitchen, drinking a cup of chocolate milk. For the first time, Milena dared to tell her about what had been happening for years. Her aunt was furious when she heard Milena recount the sordid deeds her "dear husband could never have committed." Milena ran from the kitchen to hide in the closet. Her aunt began smashing dishes against the kitchen floor. And later, crying, pulling at her hair with her hands, she called her sister-in-law and ordered flatly: "Come and pick up your daughter. We don't want her here anymore." Her mother's reaction was no different. She slapped Milena several times through her tears, saying, "But my brother wouldn't do such a thing, you stupid girl. Why would you make up something like that?" Milena had clearly ruined everything: now there was no chance her aunt and uncle would pay for her to attend middle school and high school in the city.

Milena steps back and frees herself from the hips pressing against her, leaving space for another woman in front of the mirror. Calmer than before, but still a little weak in the knees, she walks toward her table by the window. The waitress pours more coffee in her cup and smiles at this poor young woman with sad eyes.

*   *   *

In the months before she finally told her aunt, her uncle had grown bolder. He no longer hid behind the pretense of the tickling game – and it wasn't just a finger anymore. At night, he came into Milena's bedroom and lay next to her on the bed. She pretended to be asleep. Her uncle tried to stay silent, fighting the urge to scream as his mouth filled with pleasure. Milena learned to transport herself to the stillness of the closet. There her mind went blank. She could leave her body and watch what was happening from the outside, feeling nothing. She saw the pale body of a girl frozen under the brown mass of a man. Each time he panted more intensely until, spent, he fixed his flannel pants and hurried out of the dark bedroom. Only then could Milena go back to bed and try to take shelter in her body, cocooned under the sheets and blankets that failed to warm her.

*   *   *

Outside the window, the city has come back to life. The sky has cleared, and the people have returned to the streets. They step gingerly, trying to avoid the puddles that will stay there for a few days. The sun peeps out from behind the fleeing clouds and begins to warm the afternoon air. Milena asks for the bill, finishes her coffee, puts away her magazine, leaves a tip, and springs to her feet. Two tables away, the couple carries on as before, still playing the same roles: he talks and caresses his coffee cup; she listens and nibbles at her *tres leches* cake. The man pauses to takes a long swig of his coffee, and Milena bumps against his sturdy body – a sadly familiar body. Hot coffee splashes on his chest, legs, and crotch.

Milena walks away without saying a word, ignoring the man's furious shouts. She can't hear anything. A flicker of a smile crosses her face, like a ray of light that comes in slowly through a window that has just been opened.

Kisses on the Forehead

The song of the skinny Spaniard lingers in your mind. In his cigarette-hoarsened voice, he sings the story of an ugly girl who is "condemned to be chaste" and only receives "kisses on her forehead." And if she's older and heavier, you think, her fate will be even worse. "It won't be me. Today it won't be the same," you repeat again and again, as if chanting a mantra to exorcise the demons conjured up by Joaquín Sabina's song.

As your eyes dart around the plaza, you give yourself strict instructions: suck in your belly, raise your chin, take a deep breath, have confidence in yourself, keep calm. He could be one of those men striding along at a steady pace, or perhaps one of those walking with quick, quiet, pensive steps. But no. No one is wearing a red carnation, the sign you suggested and which he agreed to in his last letter. His approval of your slight eccentricity was what won you over. Anyone else would have laughed at the idea, would have called you corny and old-fashioned. But not him. Because he's special, unique. That's why you won't end up like the girl in the song. Everything will be different.

You fidget on the bench, adjusting your enormous derriere and straightening your "amply proportioned" back; "amply proportioned" was how you'd described yourself in the personal ad you placed in the magazine for women of the world:

A mature, intelligent woman, amply proportioned, wishes to meet a gentleman aged between 30-60, with serious intentions, to share long moonlit walks, stimulating conversations, glasses of wine by candlelight, and maybe the rest of our lives. Write to the following address…

Only God knows how long you hesitated before you decided to place the ad. And only the pigeons in the plaza, deprived of your daily offerings of bread and hard tortillas for almost a week, have any idea how many crumpled drafts went into the trash basket. It wasn't easy to write a description of yourself. You couldn't lie or exaggerate, but you had to twist the truth to your advantage and appear to be a good catch for a gentleman who, like you, is in search of eternal love. You managed to disguise your real intentions with ambiguous romanticism. The final version seemed sincere and convincing. The stamps on the white envelope carried saliva and the longings of a lifetime.

A lifetime… the hands of your watch, a delicate gold watch passed down from your grandmother, seem to be stuck in the cobweb of time. It's true, you got there early so you could watch him arrive. But waiting is a snail that never moves fast enough. The bench next to the kiosk, in front of the brothel, *La Casa de Naná* – this is the meeting point you suggested. You chose the place out of habit; you have sat there every evening for years. The meeting place was also a kind of test – if he recognized the location, it would suggest he was familiar with the brothel and had been there before. If he had asked you for directions, on the other hand, you would take it as proof of his chastity. The sun begins to soften and the bells clang – with disgust? – calling for six o'clock Mass. Your watch, now punctual and exact, marks the time at this moment. Time. A cold current of anxiety fills your body. The sensation is familiar to you: it's the same feeling you had when you were dropped off at school for the first time.

Until then, everything had been peace and quiet. The earth revolved as usual. But one day your mother took you to the local elementary school and left you at the gate, telling you she would pick you up at two in the afternoon. With your lunch in a lunchbox and a backpack on your back, you stood rooted to the spot until a nun touched your shoulder with her thin, cold hand and led you to your classroom. At that moment an infinite uncertainty, the sense of being abandoned by the universe, seized your small body. Time froze, a longing without end, like the rest of the day. The inevitability of the unknown. Total fear. You could never forget that sensation, though you've done a good job of hiding it in the remote drawers of your memory. Until now.

A hand, this time big and warm, touches your shoulder. He looks down at you, with his lion-like mane – a lion who has spent many years with a traveling circus. You can't make out his expression beneath the filth on his face. It's impossible to know the shade of his skin. White, brown, olive? Nor can you place a bet on his clothing – there's an indefinable reddish tint, maybe a black faded by the sun, and possibly an extremely dirty white. As your eyes travel over him, you're dumbfounded: the pigeons have petrified in front of a sunflower seed on the ground; the devout women clasp their hands in an eternal prayer; the working girls of the brothel freeze in the act of cheap, fast sex. There's been some kind of misunderstanding... then you spot a withered carnation in the buttonhole of what seems to be a frayed jacket, and your hope melts away in the heat of the evening. There's a stench of sweat and years of shabbiness emanating from your date.

"Lovely Ludivina. I knew you would arrive on time for our date. You're more beautiful than I imagined. Now my days as a Don Juan looking for a Doña Inés are over. A renowned poet said that a woman is the same book everywhere, but there are luxurious editions – like you."

Under the spell of his words, the inexplicable happens: you make your way to a motel whose walls are stained with urine and lewdness, where you agree to pick up the bill for an hour's room rental. He takes your arm and you both make your way to the stairs. While you go up, you wonder, at every step, why you're about to go to bed with a man you loathe with all your senses. Is it because you're afraid of dying without experiencing this thing they described to you as something vile? If sex turns out to be something dirty, then all those disapproving voices – your parents, the nuns, everybody – were right.

And now you lie down on a filthy bed with a scarecrow of a man who surely spends his days begging for change on some cruise ship while he delouses himself. Something urges you to abandon yourself under his skinny body, and you let him touch you with his long, blackened nails. Today, after a little more than five decades of chastity, you're living through your first love affair. You can't, however, hold back a tear when the man kisses you chastely, like a virtuous priest, on your forehead.

Peaches

Grandma Lulú's house is right in the center of the city. It is old, mysterious, and made of cantera stone, as grandparents' houses should be. The cool rooms have a view of the patio, and in the garden canaries fill the air with their yellow chirps. In the afternoons the kitchen turns into a gathering place for daughters, aunts, and daughters-in-law, who play cards with the grandma, eat cookies baked by the Carmelite nuns, and drink coffee as they gossip about the events of the day.

"Did you know that Chiquis Campuzano's daughter is getting married?" asks Aunt Delfina, sipping her coffee. She takes a cookie, nibbles it slowly, and sweetens her words with morbid curiosity and cinnamon. "I'm telling you, that girl has a bun in the oven."

The other women nod their heads greedily, urging Aunt Delfina to spill the whole story and leave out none of the details.

Above all, they're dying to hear her critiques and judgments. At that moment, unable to resist the impulse to play the good hostess, the grandma breaks into the narrator's yarn at the beginning and offers the gathering of women "more coffee, more cookies, my girls. Help yourselves to quince jelly if you like." The aunts and daughters-in-law replenish their plates and cups in preparation for an afternoon of gossip – a delightful opportunity to escape for a few hours from the tedium of housework and their unbearable husbands. Suddenly, one of the aunts asks rhetorically, "Where are the boys?" as if she felt obliged to worry. A calm silence envelops the women and no one answers because everyone knows where the boys are: they're spending energy as if youth were burning their guts out and they had to get rid of it as soon as possible. They go racing down the hall, passing through corridors and dark rooms with white walls until they reach the patio, the backyard, and finally the garden. They kick the soccer ball around and form rival teams with cousins and friends on the street. They play out furious games in which they pretend to be their favorite soccer stars. Or they might also be tormenting a dog, or watching television for hours.

"And what are the girls doing?" Again, it's Aunt Rosalina who poses the question.

"They're in the orchard," answers the grandma. Of course, it's always very important to know where the girls are. "They're picking fruit; I told them I would show them how to make pies tomorrow."

A calm "ah," with a touch of feigned surprise, fills the kitchen. Aunt Delfina skillfully picks up the thread of her monologue, as if she had never been interrupted.

"…so I told Chiquis Campuzano that girl was wicked since she was little. Once, while Chiquis and I were having a heart-to-heart, the girl interrupted me to ask if I knew what Kotex pads were for. Can you believe it? What a child!"

* * *

"Touch yourself there," demands Susana, the eldest cousin.

The blond girl with the thick braids obeys with a sad look. Lifting her skirt, she reveals her pink panties.

The girls are hiding under the largest fig tree, the one at the back of the orchard, beyond the peach and orange trees in the center. The mulberry tree, the quince tree, and the lemon trees guard the entrance to the orchard with their ripe and gentle fruits.

"Put the peach inside you," Susana orders again. "We all did it already. You have to do it too, so go on."

The girl stares at the fruit her cousin gives her and blinks in fear. "What if it gets stuck inside forever?" she asks.

"Nothing is going to happen to you, Delfinita," the others assure her.

Encouraged by the soft fuzz of the fruit and the curious glances of her cousins, the girl inserts the small peach into her small vagina, wets it, and pushes it out at once. The other girls watch, transfixed.

At that moment, they hear the dried leaves rustling on the ground and jump up, pretending to pick early figs from the fig trees. The footsteps halt and Grandma Lulú appears before them, smiling and with her hands on her hips.

"Have you already picked the fruit? I have chocolate bars for the girls who want to listen to a story," the old lady says, urging her granddaughters to return to the house. "They shouldn't be by themselves out here where no one can see them," she thinks to herself.

"A story of princesses, Grandma?"

"Yes, Delfinita. Princesses, fairies, and toads."

* * *

When they enter the kitchen, the girls are trailing behind Grandma Lulú like chicks following a hen. The aunts and daughters-in-law look up, stop talking, and smile at their respective daughters. Little Delfinita runs to her mother and throws her arms around her neck, offering her a charming smile.

"Mami, we put peaches in our quesadillas!" she announces proudly, her brown eyes gleaming. Doña Delfina lets out a smothered cry, her hand at her throat. Her mouth stays open for a few seconds as she tries to take in what she has heard. The rest of the women exchange discreet glances, uncertain whether to laugh at the girl's witticism or pretend to share her mother's shock. A few seconds later, Delfina blushes pink and seizes the girl violently by the arm.

"We have to go. My husband will be home soon and he gets mad if I don't have dinner ready," she says. Throwing kisses in the air by way of farewell, she forces a smile as she hurries from the kitchen. Confused, the girl follows closely behind her mother, trying not to be dragged along. When they reach the street, Doña Delfina slaps her daughter, dry and hard.

"Naughty girl! Look, you embarrassed me in front of your aunts. You know what busybodies they are!"

*   *   *

Delfinita has grown up. Time had to pass. She got pregnant by a boy from a well-known family and had to marry, just as Chiquis Campuzano's daughter had to. Only this time, Aunt Delfina is not the one telling the story. She has stopped coming to the afternoon get-togethers in Grandma Lulú's kitchen.

By now the peaches in the orchard have dried.

Lazarus

He never asked for this miracle, but he didn't say no when he was given the chance. Nor did he expect banners or a welcome-home cake. Still, he headed for the village with an almost fervent hope, wishing for hugs and kisses from those who had loved him when he was alive. He took no heed of his nakedness, the flesh half eaten away by worms, the yellowish meat hanging over shining white bones.

He hurried along, smiling a lipless smile, kicking up the dust with the bones of his heels. The moon shone faintly. A few clumsy moths fluttered around him, sprinkling the air with dust from their opaque wings. One white owl, feathers fluffed in apprehension, watched him suspiciously from a prickly pear tree brimming with fruit.

He found his home in shambles, worse than when he left it. He felt sorry for his wife, for he had left her with no one to protect or support her. Before he went into his house, he tried to freshen up a little, patting down the scruff of stiff hair that hung from his decomposing skull, and picking off a worm that had been playing hide-and-seek in what was left of his face, crawling first into a nostril and then into an eye socket. He pushed the door lightly, cursing when it creaked. Standing on tiptoe in the entrance, he awaited his happy reunion.

In the shadows of the adjacent room, next to a wan candle, his elderly mother was knitting. Her senses were dry, closed to everything, her mind blank. With the egotism of an only son, he took pleasure in the idea that his saintly mother was thinking of him. He leapt out in front of her, saying, "Mamita, it's me! Your Lazarus!"

It didn't go the way he thought it would: the old woman dropped her yarn and knitting needles; she opened her eyes so wide he could hear her sockets creak. Mouth agape, hands clawing at her chest, she slumped back in the chair and breathed her last. Nervous, he assured himself that he'd played no role in her heart attack. "She was already very old," he said to himself. "The poor lady."

He then walked with renewed hope toward what had been his conjugal bedroom. He hardly noticed the total absence of his belongings. He froze between the door and the vision unfolding before his hollow eyes: his adorable wife, the love of his life, his mournful widow, in the company of his compadre Joshua! They were breaking the Sixth Commandment, fornicating with uncommon passion, a passion she had never shown *him*, her husband by the laws of church and state. He wanted to cry, but his eyes had rotted away and no tears would fall. Instead, he had to express the depth of his grief by ripping off what was left of his eyelids.

He stumbled from the room and went out into the yard to confide his sorrows in Herod, his faithful dog. But the ungrateful

152

mutt growled furiously, threatening to bite off the little meat still hanging from his sad humanity.

Scurrying away from his former home, Lazarus knew he had no choice but to retrace his steps. On the way back, neither the moths nor the fluffed-up owl spared him a look. The road, which did not lead to Rome, soon took him to the entrance of the cemetery. He sat down on a tombstone covered with yellow grass and watched the scorpions trying to hide under the bones of his feet. On that moonless night, he truly wished he weren't living in the age of miracles.

The Curse of Eve
(A Tragedy in Seven Acts)

I

A trickle of water runs down her legs. Before she can feel ashamed, the pain comes and she calls for her mother. Between small, stifled howls, she curses her husband with the deepest and purest hatred she has ever felt in her life. If someone had warned her that this might happen, she would never have risked such misery for the promise of an orgasm. And that was all it was – a promise. A zipper zipped down, her skirt lifted up, some clumsy fiddling. His voice, ashamed: "I'm sorry, I usually last longer. I don't know what's wrong with me today." And now this.

II

The lance pierces her body for what seems an eternity. A wave of pain forces her to shut her eyes tight. The greasy white ceiling of the hospital has started to peel off, revealing an old pistachio color. The nurse, who is probably on her second shift, takes her blood pressure reluctantly, and later jams a needle into her arm as if stuffing a Christmas turkey. Another spasm of pain makes her shudder and scream. A doctor sticks his head between her legs and – continuing the yuletide simile – examines her with the nonchalance of a chef checking the turkey in the oven. He murmurs, just loudly enough for her to hear, "Ah, but the last time you opened your legs you weren't complaining." Drowning in her own pain, she can't protest. Again, the agony threatens her. As she blinks back her tears, her mother's hand caresses her sweaty forehead. Only then does she ask her mother how she got to the hospital, and where her husband is – he's the one responsible for this ordeal and he's clearly not here now. This gets her started on a bitter diatribe against men, life, and God himself, and against the injustice of finding herself in the delivery room at the age of twenty and not out drinking at a bar with her friends.

"Oh, *mija*, you're always looking for tits on snakes and sleeves on vests. You're a married woman. Having kids is your fate. The younger you start a family, the better. The first one is always difficult. After this everything gets easy, really. Take it like a woman."

III

The buoyant illusion created by the baby shower gifts – the pretty dresses and accessories for the mother-to-be and her baby – fades with the first dilated inches and a sensation that is inconceivable to anyone who hasn't lived through it. The discomforts that come with pregnancy – endless vomiting, varicose veins, insatiable hunger, difficulty sleeping or moving, cramped organs, constipation, hemorrhoids – seem like a week at the beauty spa compared with the torments of labor. She thinks she might die any minute now and lets out another howl at the height of the pain. Just as she is about to faint, her husband arrives. She grabs his lapels and hangs on with all her might. She swears to herself that if he dares to bring up the same old nonsense – "Labor is natural. All animals go through this, but they don't complain like you. Besides, our grandmothers didn't have access to sedatives or the medical advances that exist today, and they didn't whine like this" – she will strangle him without a pang of conscience. Perhaps he suspects as much; he tries to disentangle himself gently from his wife's grip. He coos, "Hang in there, my love. You're doing great."

A whole congregation seems to have clustered around her legs, and she no longer has the strength to protest. This torture, courtesy of Mother Nature, has made her lose all notions of modesty. She lets all eyes focus on her private area, which is about to split in two at any moment. When she thinks she has reached the peak of her suffering and it's not possible to feel any more pain, the doctor announces casually, "Let's cut her here to get the baby out without tearing her."

What follows next is the icing on the cake. And this time she does faint.

IV

The woman's figure was nothing spectacular, but she did have the good fortune to be relatively thin. Now, after nine months of limited movement and a daily caloric intake three times the usual amount, she has no figure at all. Sayings such as "pregnant women should rest" and "you have to satisfy all your cravings, otherwise your baby will come out with a face of…" (whatever the local superstition says) led her to gain more than forty pounds. From now on, she will walk up and down the sidewalks, pushing a stroller, clinging to the illusion that she is burning a few calories. She will be passed in the street by willowy girls with flat abdomens and surgically enhanced breasts and noses, their skimpy clothing showing off their perfect bodies – they make her sick. Nausea will make her go home and eat half a chocolate cake, and then she'll feel defeated and depressed for being so unlike her former self. She will discover, a little later, that her nausea has a cause: how quickly she forgot those first unmistakable symptoms. Her mother's tone is conciliatory – "It's better to have your second child now; that way you'll finish raising them faster. Besides, they can play together" – but nothing can comfort her as she throws herself in her mother's arms, crying, a pregnancy test in her hand: positive.

V

The present cuts into her like a scalpel. Strictly speaking, there is no incision, but her perineum opens like a flower to the touch of the sharp metal. She recovers consciousness with the fearful start of someone waking from a nightmare. She's glad to realize she'd been dreaming. The reality is an ordeal, but not nearly as distressing as that fleeting glimpse into the future, an unfortunately not-so-distant future: if she were in a marathon instead of in labor, she would now be running the last two kilometers. It's nothing compared to the forty kilometers she has already covered, but it's surely the last few that are the most exhausting. She pushes one more time with all her strength. Just as her soul and her intestines are about to escape from her sullied orifice, she crosses the finishing line. There is no sense of triumph. She is greeted by a high-pitched cry, unfamiliar, yet one which will accompany her for the next several months at all hours of the day.

VI

She would like to tell someone – anyone at all, from the hostile nurse to the young man sweeping the hospital corridor – that she feels infinitely sad. This makes her feel guilty: "The birth of a child should be a special and happy occasion in the life of every proud woman." However, she doesn't feel like seeing her baby girl – a small, mewling infant who will inherit the sufferings of her kind with the passage of time – much less the mob of friends and family who come and go from her room. Even though they bring her gifts – Trojan horses – her visitors seem like nothing more than vultures circling. Will she not have a moment's rest? Her mother-in-law has made her presence known now that the labor is over, never failing to shower her with orders and advice. She even scrutinizes the size of her breasts and determines how many minutes at a time each breast should be offered to the baby. If there is one decisive moment when an ordinary citizen turns into a mass murderer, this must be it. Every time someone enters the room with a bouquet of flowers, she is expected to offer a smile of thanks, though smiling is the last thing she feels like doing: she has the face of someone lying on a medieval battlefield; constipation; a wound in her body that threatens to break open; an unbearable burning in her breasts; and all these pounds that cling to her even though she has already given birth.

With the mob clustered around the bed in her small room – an insipid mob that doesn't stop asking questions and giving unwanted advice – it dawns on her that her husband, her sweet companion, the father of this newborn child who now makes her nipples bleed, is absent. Her mother-in-law, the resentful Jocasta who won't accept that her little Oedipus has found another woman, notices the frustration on her face and says, with a cruel smile, "Joaquincito went home to sleep. He was exhausted after waiting for so many hours, poor baby. I fixed him something to eat and tucked him into bed."

VII

Oblivious to her sharp cries, the man who swore at the altar to love her for better or worse continues to dose. For the next decade, she will never sleep a whole night through, nor have an opportunity to regain the figure she once had. Her slack and enlarged breasts will become flabby when she breastfeeds the second child. The muscles in her belly will become so weak that her subsequent pregnancies will begin to show within days of conception. Her stretch marks will multiply unashamedly. Her bones will continue to lose calcium, secretly, in silence, until one fine day she's surprised, in her lonely widowhood, by a broken hip. This life – so "fulfilling" for a woman – will turn her into a prisoner of her progeny, and all her personal needs will be nullified by the desires of her children and her husband. She will have no rest or relaxation. Her arduous and endless housework will never be relieved by a "thank you" or a helping hand. Her professional ambitions will remain as unknown and fantastic as a trip to Mars. To complete the picture, one day she will find, in her husband's jacket, some overwhelming evidence of his infidelity, which he won't deny and which he will even argue is her fault: "Look at yourself, you're a mess. Besides, you never have any time for me. Why shouldn't I find someone who pays attention to me? Someone who fixes herself up to please me?"

But she doesn't know any of this. She can't foretell the future that approaches as tragically and discretely as a tsunami. Now, as her baby looks her in the eye and grasps her thumb in her tiny hand, she's surprised to find herself shedding a single hot tear. She, a new mother, realizes that at this moment nothing else matters.